I0572351

LK Hunsaker

Also by LK Hunsaker
+_+_+

Finishing Touches

Rehearsal: A Different Drummer

Rehearsal: The Highest Aim

Off The Moon

Protect The Heart
+_+_+

A Novel

LK Hunsaker

elucidate publishing

ISBN 978-0-9825299-2-8

Cover art: LK Hunsaker

elucidate publishing
staff@elucidatepublishing.net
PO Box 1262, Hermitage PA 16137
United States of America
(we prefer email!)

electronic version available

For the Military Spouses who remain stalwart as they stand
behind their soldiers, airmen, sailors, marines, & guardsmen.

Support work is unglamorous.
It is often physically unrewarding.
It is, however, the shelter of the country's heart.
Thank you.

one

Abraham slung his backpack over his shoulders and headed down the dusty road toward town. His father asked to take him. Begged, nearly. But Abe didn't want his goodbye, which could be his final goodbye, to be at the train depot. He wanted it at home, on their farm, where by all rights he should have been helping with chores. His father would manage without him. He had always managed. Even through the torturous years of watching Abraham's mother drift away through the mind-dissolving dementia and then finally leave them for good, his father had managed.

Abraham hoped with every part of his soul he would return to the farm, to his father, and be there to help him manage during his aging days. It would be soon. Charles Luchner showed signs of slowing. It hurt Abe to see it. It would hurt him more to have to see his father watch him leave on that train, standing on the platform managing to control his sadness, his fear.

At the edge of his property, he kicked a rock out of his path. The long walk into town would do him good, help him prepare for what was to come. Not that he wasn't prepared already. Constant farm chores without machinery to make them easier had built his strength and stamina well. Days of rising before the roosters to take care of the crops and the cows, and to move lines in bitter cold air and knee deep snow and in the hottest times of the summer made him sturdy. He didn't figure war would be much harder, physically. What he wasn't sure of was how disruptive it would be to his mind. He had no qualm about fighting as needed. He was raised to stand up for himself and those around him and did so without hesitation. And now he was proud to do it for his country. He'd never actually taken a life, though. He knew how to avoid that risk during a fight.

His father told him to be someone else out there, to tell himself he was doing good and that sometimes evil was necessary to prevent worse evil. *"Never let it make you feel bad about who you are."* Charles Luchner's voice echoed in his thoughts. *"Remember your heart is in the right place and that's what matters."* Lives came and went. They always would. The heart is what lasted. Protect the heart, he'd said.

Abraham adjusted his backpack in an imitation of adjusting his thoughts and wondered how soon his father would find the wood carving at the back side of the house. He'd done it in secret as a message for when he wasn't there. A heart. Enclosed within hands inside an image of the farm, their farm. Abe engraved it in the back of the wooden bench swing he'd made while he kept it hidden in a corner of the barn. His father loved to sit out behind the house on nice days and simply look over their land, land passed through generations of his family, worked by many hands who loved their bit of America, as his father said. Before he left, Abe wanted him to have a more comfortable place to do it; a place that would leave a part of himself behind for his father to keep. He'd moved it out to the yard just as dawn was breaking.

As he walked, he eyed the light echo of misty mountains in the distance. There weren't many trees in Snake River country, at least not in his part of it, in southern Idaho. What were there were rather sparse, as compared to what he'd seen during his travels back east. His father had sent him to see something of the country after he earned his diploma and before he settled in to learn how to take over the farm. Abraham's thoughts often returned to the long train trip where he jumped off here and there to explore different territories and different people. As much as he loved the travel, he also loved the return to his mountains. To his farm. One day, it would be his. One day after that, he would share it with a family of his own. Anyway, that was his plan.

If he returned.

Tires flying up the gravel road from behind broke his thoughts and he moved into the yellowed weeds. They needed rain. But then, they usually needed rain.

The car stopped. "Get in."

Abe sighed and looked over at Cameron. He wanted the long walk into town to be alone with his thoughts, to be alone in the circle of his mountains.

"Come on. What're you walking for, anyway? Old man wouldn't take you in?"

"He tried. Go on. I'll meet you in town."

"Have you lost your marbles? Don't think we'll get enough walking when we're shipped out? Get in." Cameron reached over to open the passenger door.

It would be pointless to argue. His friend was too stubborn. Abe threw his pack in the back seat and lowered into the front.

"So this should be some grand adventure, hey?" Cam threw the car back into gear and skidded the gravel. "A few nights in town and then off on a hero's journey. Can't wait to show up at Maura's in this uniform. Bet she'll give in to me when she sees it's going to be real. Don't you bet?"

"Don't know, Cam. Haven't met her but from what you've said, I'd have my doubts."

"Aw, but she's just scared I won't come back, you know. And when she sees that could really be, when I show up looking like a real soldier, she'll wanta make sure we at least have a couple days. Right?"

Abraham didn't bother to answer. Nothing he said would matter. If Cameron hadn't taken Maura's hints by now, more than hints from the way it sounded, he wouldn't take them from Abe, either. The girl didn't want a soldier. She wanted someone who would be around. Abe couldn't blame her.

"So come on up to her place with me. You should meet, you know. It's about time you did, as you're my best friend and she's my best girl…"

"I'm your only friend, and my guess is she's not your only girl, which could be part of her objection."

Cam laughed. "That's Abe. Always too blunt. No wonder you don't have a girl. They don't like that. You gotta learn to sweet talk."

"Some girl might want blunt instead of roundabout truths that sound good."

"Yeah, maybe. But not the kind I want." He turned a corner too sharp.

Abe grabbed the dash. "Why are you in uniform already? We aren't supposed to be. Not till we're officially signed and sworn."

"Didn't you hear me at all? I'm going to go sweep my gal off her feet. Gotta look real."

Maybe you should be *real instead*. Abe didn't say it. He knew he should say it. But he didn't. Instead, he watched the horizon, the tumbleweeds drifting in the browned flat fields, the cows in the dairy farm they passed with its odor lingering along with them. The town was barely within his view now, the grain silo at its edge a beacon of sorts.

The day before, he'd spent time along the canyon, wandering its edge, peering down the jagged rocks where not much more than a trickle of water snaked along the bottom of the wide crevice. There wasn't much water this time of year. The way the little bit of it that went through had dredged such a huge canyon in its wake was a magical thing in Abe's mind. He'd carved images of it now and then, in tree trunks that ended up shaped like the canyon, at least to some extent. One of them he'd sold to a bank in town. They'd topped it with a piece of thick glass, put the thing on legs, and used it as a welcome table just inside the entrance, complete with a plaque stating the "artist's" name.

Abe didn't feel like an artist and so it was kind of embarrassing when people made note of it and asked him what he'd done recently. He liked wood. He liked working with his hands. He loved nature. And so the wood carvings just slipped out. He'd sold a couple of other pieces, smaller, that became wall hangings or shelf decorations. He didn't charge much. His father said he should increase his price, as much as people liked his work. But he would do it even if no one bought it, so he figured getting a few dollars here and there for things he didn't know what to do with as he finished them was good enough.

He had packed his carving tools, though. He hoped they'd be allowed to travel with him. If not, he'd drop them by the bank to be returned to his father next time he was in town.

Charles Luchner would have to go to town more often since Abe wasn't there to go for him. The thought made his heart heavy. Father didn't like going into town, not since Mother had become not herself and people start to stare and treat her differently. Father couldn't see those people without it reminding him.

Abe wasn't bothered by it. They were only concerned or confused. Or maybe they were afraid if it could happen to such a beautiful, intelligent soul as Annette Luchner, it could just as easily happen to them and they didn't want to face it. Maybe going into town on a regular basis would be good for his father. He needed to talk to people more, other than the few long-time friends who stopped by or whom he visited. Abe was at least glad his father would still have them.

"Hey, hello. Why do I think I'm talking to myself?"

Abe threw a questioning gaze at Cam as the car came to a stop in front of a diner.

"Didn't hear a word I said, did you? You gotta stop that, Abe, or people will think you're going nuts already like your mother. You're too young for that. Although I know it's just 'cause you're too into your own thoughts. Others won't know."

"She wasn't nuts." He opened the door, got out, and grabbed his pack from the back. "I'll meet up with you…"

"Hey, come on. I know she wasn't." Cam caught up and took his arm. "Put it back for now." He gripped Abe's pack and threw it in the car. "We're going to eat. I plan to eat hearty the next few days while I can and you're going to join me."

"I ate before I left."

"Yeah, sure ya did. But I mean really eat. Thick steak. Beer. The whole thing. We deserve this. And I'm buying so don't argue."

"No need for that. I've got money saved."

"I know you do, but my guess is I'll need favors before long so I'm paying for them now."

"I'm your friend, Cam. You don't have to buy my favors."

A woman walking past threw a surprised glance at his statement.

Cam laughed. "Great, now we're even more hooked together in their minds. Buy my favors. What a riot. That'll be everywhere by tonight."

With a sigh, Abe knew his friend was right. But they all knew Abe well. It would be no more than a laugh, even if they weren't so sure of Cameron.

His family was new in the area, up from somewhere in California, and Cameron's rash decisions and joking nature made it hard for locals to understand him. Without understanding him, they couldn't quite accept him into their midst other than with the general friendliness they showed everyone.

It didn't help matters that Cameron's family dressed their part. They had money. So did lots of folks around, but most didn't show it. They were farmers, hatchery owners, store managers, and so on, but you had to know who had the money in order to tell. They all dressed casual and comfortable, ready for work at the drop of a hat. Of course, the bankers and such were dressed for the job, but still, you'd be hard-pressed to tell an owner from a teller if you didn't know.

Abe appreciated that. So did the rest of the area. Cam's family showed too much, boasted too much. Dressed nice just to grocery shop. Because of it, few locals gave them more courtesy than the time of day.

Cam chose a table front and center, shoulders back boasting in his uniform he shouldn't have been wearing. It worked, though. Everyone stopped to talk to him at least long enough to wish him well and a safe return. They wished Abe well, also, even if he wasn't in uniform. They all knew.

Maura set the warm plate on the table in front of her father and kissed his head. "Your favorite today, Papa. Fried ham and fresh corn. Make sure you eat that banana, too, to counter the salt."

"The corn isn't on the cob. I like it on the cob."

"I know you do, but it hurts your teeth. Remember? This is fresh from the cob. I cut it off. It's the same corn."

"It's not on the cob."

Maura sighed. "Yes, I know. I'm sorry. But please eat well today. Mrs. Jacobs will be here soon to check on you. I'm off to the home now. I won't be late."

"Mrs. Jacobs smells like alcohol. She drinks." He teased the corn with his fork prongs.

"She doesn't drink, Papa. She's a nurse. She uses alcohol to clean the equipment and people's arms before they get shots. Be nice to her, please. I'll be back soon."

"I don't know why you spend your time at that place. You'll catch something one of these days and then what'll I do?"

Maura left him rambling. He would likely go on for the next ten minutes about why she shouldn't volunteer her time at the women and children's home. She heard it on a near-daily basis, but it kept her hands and mind occupied. And she loved taking care of the little ones, the infants especially. Someone had to do it. Her father said they got themselves into the mess, they should get themselves out. Maybe it was true. Sometimes. But sometimes it wasn't their fault. Many were war widows, young war widows left with children. The older women could usually find jobs to pay their own expenses. Those with children weren't often hired, and if they were, they had nowhere to take the babies while they worked. They did their best. It often wasn't enough.

Even with those for whom it was out of lack of responsibility, as her father yelled about, it was because they weren't taught well, so she figured. As she worked with them, Maura tried to help them see how to prevent further hardships for themselves. She wasn't sure it ever worked.

It got her out of her father's house, anyway, and gave her a break from the way he consistently asked of Cameron. When he was coming next. When he would propose already as a gentleman should. Maura couldn't tell him Cameron had proposed. She couldn't accept. Not now. Not until he came back. She'd seen enough war widows struggle to get by. She had no intention of being one of them. No. She would stay with her father and put up with being his main caregiver for now. And she would do something worthwhile in the meantime, while she waited. Not that she saw the war ending any time soon. but she hoped it did before she'd be considered too much a spinster for anyone to still be interested. Even if she was older than most, she would be unencumbered, with no little ones of her own for a man to have to take care of, as well. She expected that would work in her favor.

Part of her felt traitorous to Cameron for even thinking about other men, but then, she hadn't exactly chosen him. He chose her. He'd simply asked her father for permission to come around now and then and had taken to doing so. Maura enjoyed his company. He was nice enough. His humor made her laugh, and laughing these days was a privilege. Her father liked that he had money so she would be taken care of well.

Maura couldn't imagine herself actually being taken care of. She'd always done well enough with that on her own, on top of taking care of others. Her mother. Maura had taken full care of her until she was gone. Now she had her father. And the orphans and widows, and sometimes a soldier who came back wounded they let stay in a far part of the building away from the widows. Not that they didn't find ways to mingle.

Maura did not mingle. If they were in the home, they needed help to care for themselves. She was glad to do it at work, but enough was enough. Dealing with her father was enough. She didn't need another man to support.

That was one reason Cameron appealed to her. Maybe he did have money, but he also worked hard. She'd seen him in shirt-tails coming into town with that friend of his to get farm supplies. She never approached him at those times, but she watched him. He had a nice build, nearly a match of his friend's. They could almost have been brothers except for what she knew of their personalities. Abraham was awfully quiet. He hardly talked to people. That, and the way the town talked about his wood crafts was all she knew of him. And he also had care of his father on his own. Unlike Maura's, though, Abraham's father was still able to work and care for himself.

With another sigh, she grasped her parasol from the rack beside the front door and went out to the front porch. She didn't want it opened to cover her head. The sun leaked beautiful heat from the sky and she wanted to raise her face and let it sink in. Her father would have a fit. Young women of "a certain class" shouldn't look like farm hands. Did he think if she did marry Cameron, she wouldn't ever help him on the farm? She supposed the wealthier farm ladies didn't, but the thought appealed to her, maybe even more than Cameron did. She had to think caring for crops and animals would be much like working at the home in care of people, but with less heartache. The infants she always fell in love with were adopted out easily if they were open for adoption. The young mothers often settled for whatever man would have them and their children, often older men they didn't care anything about. It hurt her to see it.

No. Maura wouldn't be one of them. She would wait. If she didn't find someone, she would be fine on her own. The house would go to her when her father passed. She could take care of herself as long as she had a roof over her head.

Pausing at the trellis, she fingered a morning glory and dropped the parasol back to allow the dense blue-spotted vine to provide her shade. Its soft silky petal felt much like an infant's cheek. Delicate and yet hardy. Calming and nurturing even as it needed to be nurtured. Her mother said, when they had last sat on the front porch together, how the morning glories reminded her of Maura. Each year the plant rejuvenated itself, became more hearty, more filled in, with more blooms.

Maybe her mother was right, but she felt more like her beloved columbine with their two layers in two shades, one softly rounded, the other pointed, as if in warning. The yellow stamen shooting so proudly from the center announced their need and longing for pollination. Maura blushed at the thought. She was, after all, old enough. Twenty-three already. Quite old enough.

"Good afternoon, Miss Laerty."

She jumped at Cameron's voice, amazed she hadn't noticed his car pull in front of her house as she stood admiring her flowers. Maura shoved the indecent thoughts out of her mind while she faced him. "Oh, good afternoon, Mr. Terry. You aren't off already, are you?" She couldn't help but stare at Cameron in his olive green uniform. It made her heart hurt. She didn't want him to come back like those men at the other end of the home. With his risk-taking and high spirits, she was awfully afraid he would.

"I have nearly two full days yet. Abe and I are in town to get ready is all. Thought I would start getting used to it." He stepped out and offered his arm. "I hoped to take you for a walk around town."

"I'm afraid I have plans."

"You have plans?" He looked alarmed.

"Yes. I was on my way to the home. They're expecting me today."

"Oh." His face relaxed. "Well, I don't suppose I could change your mind, seeing as I have only two days left and all?"

"For now. Two days left for now, you mean, Mr. Terry. And I expect you to come home walking, by the way. You do know I expect that."

He bowed. "I will do my best to accommodate you."

His grin was too charming. She had to pull her eyes away. "I do need to go in to the home for a bit, but I suppose I could leave early. Would you like to come for dinner? Father would enjoy the extra company."

"I would be honored. Please, allow me to drive you and I'll pick you up after if you'll give me a time."

Maura couldn't refuse. After all, Cameron was leaving. She might as well enjoy the company, also, while she could. "You are welcome to bring your friend along, if you would like. You say he's in town with you?"

"Abe? Yes, he's in town. But he has 'errands' to take care of, so he says. Trying to make sure everything is set for his father while he's away, I believe. I told him I'd have my younger brothers stop by now and then to offer help. He seems to appreciate it, but he still worries."

"His father is in good health, though, I hear."

"Oh yes. For a man nearly sixty, he is in good health. They are close, however, and Abe worries he will work too hard there alone. Not like you and your father or me and my own, where we put up with each other only as we are related by circumstance. If anything happens to Abe, the old man will be devastated. His world centers on him."

"Lord willing he won't be away long, then. Or you."

Cameron lifted her hand to kiss her fingers.

She blushed. "We're in public. What will people think?"

"They'll think you're inclined to become my wife. As I'm inclined to think you might, also."

"Mr. Terry…"

"Please, Maura. Cameron. At least do me the favor of using my first name and allowing me use of yours."

"I believe you have already taken that liberty."

He grinned. "And I believe you are starting to bend to my request. But we'll talk more of it later, after dinner tonight when we take a stroll."

"Cameron." His name was hard for Maura to say. It seemed improper. Of course it shouldn't since they were courting and it wasn't a secret they were courting. Still...

"Don't say more." He pressed a finger against her lips.

Maura cast her eyes along the dark sidewalk. They were beneath a street lamp, too easily seen. She would have to accept him if she allowed such contact. She pulled back. "Please don't."

"Maura. I wish for you to be my wife. Not when I return, but now. Before I leave. I want to know you are here waiting for my arms. We can be married tomorrow. And then we will have our wedding night to help..."

"Don't." Her voice was a whisper. "I can't." She should tell him. She should simply say she was not yet sure he was right for her. It felt too cruel. "Cameron, I simply can't do it. I can't become your wife and then wonder if it was only for a night, if you'll come back or if..."

"Or if I get injured and you no longer want me." His voice was harsh.

"No. It's not what I meant."

"Isn't it?"

She turned away. Maybe she did, in part. Was it cruel? If she'd loved him enough, she wouldn't think twice on accepting him now, accepting what would come. She didn't. The thought of a wedding night with Cameron didn't settle well in her soul. If she wanted him, truly wanted him, she would feel differently.

"Well then." Cameron stiffened and turned toward her house. "We shall wait. But I will overlook this. And when I return, I will ask again for your hand, whether or not I am quite the same man I am now. Then we shall see if it is not what you meant."

Something in his tone unsettled her worse than the thought of a wedding night. Maura accepted his arm and walked back down the dark sidewalk, up to her front porch. "Will you come in?"

"I think I won't, thank you. This shall be my goodbye to you. For now. I do hope it is not long before we meet again." He kissed her hand. "Be well, Maura. I shall see you in my mind just like this every night before I sleep."

Her eyes misted. "Be well, Cameron. And do come home safe."

He gave her a light nod and stepped backward.

She stopped him and wrapped her arms around his waist; her head fell to his shoulder. "I do care for you. Please know that. I am only afraid…"

"I know, my love. I had hoped to make you less afraid. Remember, some of us do return." He planted a kiss aside her head. "May I write to you?"

"Of course. Please." She raised her eyes to his. "Yes, do write to me. I will answer."

"I will look for your letters every day." He released himself from her arms and gave her a light bow. "Good night, Miss Laerty. Until then."

Maura watched him stride to his car, open the door, and climb swiftly inside. He gave her a wave as he pulled off. Her heart fell. Was she wrong to turn him away?

No. She was right. She would not end up as those women in the home.

three

Abe felt someone approach the table and set a finger beside the paragraph he was trying to read through the noise of the inn's common room. Cameron had daydreamed through the briefing and would, in all likelihood, leave his own manual untouched. It would be up to Abe to make sure his friend knew whatever he could sneak into the conversation at opportune times.

"Good evening, Mr. Luchner."

With a start, he shoved his chair back, rose to his feet, and gave Sadie a light nod. "Miss Monroe." He allowed only the slightest glance at her modest gown, a reddish-purple thing with little accessory and no lace. Abraham had never seen Sadie Monroe wear lace. "How are you this evening?"

"I am afraid I am not in high spirits. Are you going to offer me a chair?"

"My apologies." Holding it for her, Abe kept his gaze away from her low-cut bodice and moved back to his own seat. "May I ask if anything is wrong for your spirits to be low? Is your mother well?"

"Mother is well enough. I no longer allow her moods to dictate my own."

"I am glad to hear." He tensed under her amused expression. "That is to say, I am glad she is well. Can I offer you anything? An iced tea, perhaps? It is a warm night."

"Thank you. No." She twisted the end of a brunette strand between her fingers. "I only wondered if you might enjoy company this evening. You look dreadfully alone, and you should not be with where you are headed. It is, of course, why I am not in high spirits. I've no idea when we might see each other again."

"It is impossible to say." Abe cast his eyes to the far side of the room where Cameron ordered another whiskey and laughed with one of the bar maids. "I do well alone, however. You needn't worry."

"Oh. I'm bothering you, then."

"No." He only meant he didn't need a bar maid in lieu of her companionship. He supposed he wouldn't be so forward with his thoughts. "Your company is always pleasant. I simply meant..."

She took his hand. "Abraham, I understand what you meant. I'm only teasing. Wouldn't you like to go for a stroll? The air is lovely."

He considered accepting. Another evening of Sadie's lively spirit and pretty smile would be a nice way to spend his last night in town, but he had to decline. "Thank you. I'm rather tired tonight and plan to head upstairs early."

"Abe." She leaned closer. "Let me keep you from being so lonely before you leave. What you're walking into … it makes me proud, but it worries me. I'm afraid I won't see you again and I'm not so bold on normal occasions, but you must know I have interest and I will gladly wait…"

"Miss Monroe, you mustn't…" He backed away before he would be beholden to her.

"And why mustn't I? It's the truth."

"It's not appropriate. I'm leaving and I cannot promise I'll return. I will not be unfair enough to ask you to…"

"But you're not asking." She stroked his hand with her soft fingers. "Is there another? A girl who has your heart enough you will not look my way longer than a moment?"

"There is no other. I will not leave with entanglements."

"Oh, but Abraham, wouldn't you be happier knowing someone waits for you? Wouldn't it help you be more careful and fight harder to come home?"

"My father will need my help on the farm as he grows older. Anything otherwise, I believe, would be only a distraction. A distraction I do not need or wish to have." He took his hand away and stood. "I must ask beg of your leave. Please look after yourself, Miss Monroe."

Courteous or not, he left her there at the table and strode up the stairs to the room he shared with Cameron. Opening the book again, Abe threw his thoughts into where he was headed. It was why he wanted the two days in town away from home before he left: to put himself into his new position, to ready himself as near as was possible.

He covered his eyes at the sudden light and click of the door.

"I didn't mean to wake you."

"What time is it?" Abe could hardly see Cameron between the sudden light and a blur as his friend wobbled over to drop on his bed.

"Morning sometime, I would say. What a glorious night it was."

Abe dropped back onto his pillow. "I suppose, then, you have been with your girl and she agreed to your proposal?"

"My girl." Cameron laughed. "My girl is the most beautiful in the world, she is."

"Then there is to be a wedding tomorrow?"

"Wedding." He dropped his arm over top his face and muffled his voice. "No wedding. Not until I am returned again, she said. Trusting girl. The most beautiful in the world."

Abraham didn't for a moment believe it was Cameron's girl he'd spent the night with. More likely the bar maid. He couldn't help a sigh.

+_+_+ Fall +_+_+

four

"There is a letter for you. I placed it on the buffet."

"I'll look later, Father. Thank you." Maura slipped out of her shoes and heavy wrap. Evenings were cool now with September's entrance. Her asters had a few blooms and the mums were becoming lively and vivid. It was time to put in the fall crops: broccoli, cabbage, cauliflower, parsnip. Her weary limbs refused the thought. There was too much work to do at the home. The other side of the building filled much too fast. Boys returning. Needing extra care. Yelling out their nightmares. It sapped her strength, wrenched her insides.

"You'll want this one, I expect." Her father leaned against his cane as he approached. "Maura, you work too hard. It is not healthy."

"I'm fine, Papa. I'm much healthier than those boys who need my assistance. And the children. Oh, there are so many now." She shoved a strand of hair back from where it fell out of her bun.

"You should not weary yourself so. Your Mr. Terry will turn away when he comes back and sees you bedraggled."

With a sigh, she lowered onto the chaise. "If that is the case, he is free to turn away."

"Is that so? Then you'll not want the letter. I'll throw it in the rubbish pile."

It was as well if he did. Her weary eyes wouldn't appreciate the attempt to read. She'd spent plenty of time reading earlier, to boys with bandaged eyes and hands, to help entertain them as they recovered. Reading aloud tired her. Even back in the days of learning, when the class took turns…

It took four clops of her father's cane in retreat before Maura realized what he meant. A letter from Cameron? Three months had passed since his leaving. Maura expected he had given up with her refusal. Much of her wished it was true. It would be easier if the worst happened.

But if there was word…

She rushed to catch up and grasped the letter from the large-knuckled and wrinkled fingers. The postmark dated three weeks earlier. It had taken far too long to arrive. "I'll get to dinner in a bit, Papa. I need to rest my feet a moment first."

"Yes. Rest your feet. Be sure to let me know what Mr. Terry has to say, if you will. I would be there myself if I could."

Maura yanked her gaze from the dirty envelope to her father's face. "And why would you wish to go back again after you've done your part?"

"What is there more important, my daughter, then protecting a way of life that provides so many blessings, and that so many before have fought to protect?"

"Yes Papa, I know, but once should be enough for anyone."

"It may be, but many times it is not. You are young yet. You shall see." With a pat to her hand, he hobbled away to the parlor and his favorite chair.

Maura studied the handwriting on the envelope. It was elegant and wild all at once, a reminder of Cameron's personality. She couldn't help a light grin as she made her way to her room. Before she would read it, she wanted to be out of her decent things and into her house dress for comfort. Hanging the heavy garment on the rod, she wrapped into her old frock Papa said she should be rid of, retrieved the letter, and pulled her afghan over her legs.

She used her opener carefully and ripped only the top edge. She didn't want any of his words, even on the envelope, sundered.

An odd scent wafted up from the pages inside: similar to dirt but different, something she had never smelled and couldn't describe. Maura held it to her nose to absorb the new odor, allowing it to seep into her own experience and take her elsewhere, wherever Cameron was. She didn't know precisely. She knew it was a different world, that the view it gave him would entrench something into his soul she would never fully understand. The miles in distance could never compete with the separation of experience.

Perhaps it would be good for him, for them. Her feelings for him could be stronger with his change. They could also lessen.

She wouldn't think of it. There was no reason to think of it until he returned. They would take it from that point forward and allow it to progress. Or not.

With another sigh, Maura opened her eyes and unfolded the papers. The first page was a drawing, a simple sketch of tents, and of mountains, not like those around her but jagged, harsh, rocky instead of tree-covered. A man crouched over a fire. It was a good likeness of Cameron's build. The neat initials nearly hidden behind the backpack read: AL.

She set the drawing carefully to her side where she could see it and leaned back, letting her body meld with the lounge.

Dearest Maura,

With many apologies, I send this letter. I had meant to write upon first arrival in expectation, that, since you would have my address with the letter, I could look forward to receiving yours. I was unprepared for the reality that would be the first two months of Army life, however. We have been on the move nearly without stop and we train every spare minute. When we are not moving or training, it has become a necessity to sleep. Sleep is rare. And highly valued. Not more highly valued than you are, my dear one, but nearly as high. Today is the first day I have been able to sit on my bunk without falling into a deep coma. So please, allow me your forgiveness.

If you would, I have enclosed a sketch my friend and savior, Abraham, did one night while restless. I ask if you would pass it along to Miss Sadie Monroe, who has an especial fondness for him, along with this address she can use to write.

I'm afraid I make a horrendous subject matter. However, I thought it might amuse Miss Monroe to see how he keeps his hands busy out here where he seems very much in his element. A good soldier, Abe is. Confident and knowledgeable. I am more pleased than I can tell you to have him at my side trying to teach me to be the soldier he is. I fear I will never come up to that level, but the attempt is admirable, on his part and on my own, if I can say as much.

Dear Maura, I am afraid this must be a short letter, as I grow weary and sleep grows in fondness. I will so look forward to your return letter, as you promised. I am a cad to ask it to be longer than my own, but I do pray you are not tiring yourself too far and will therefore have the strength for the task. Do tell me of the home and of your father and of any news of pertinence around town. Even news of no important nature would be welcome.

My very best wishes to you always.
Yours,
Cameron

Maura studied the drawing she was to give Miss Monroe and wiped dampness from around her eyes. He was well, although tired. Confident and knowledgeable. His friend was. She sent up a quick prayer for them both, for Cameron to learn well and to remain safe. Also for Abraham who looked after him.

She did not want to give the drawing away. It was sent to her. She should be able to keep it even if it was Abraham's work. It was of Cameron and was sent to her. With a sigh, she knew she would pass it along as asked. She couldn't tell him she refused to do so.

five

Abraham pulled his boots off and set them beside his bunk. Blisters lined the sides of his feet, but he refused to give them notice. He was tired of walking. Tired of sand sifting into every part: between his toes, under his arms, in his hair and down his back. As the weather began to cool, he spent less time drenched in sweat that made the sand extra gritty. His skin was less raw. Soon, they said, the temperature would drop and they would wish for days of sweat. Although he believed it was true, for the moment, he would gladly accept any bit of cool he could get.

Fighting wasn't heavy where they were. He was at least glad of that. They had few casualties and none from his unit. As he could, he stayed close to Cameron. His friend's aim was good. His problem was in keeping his head involved enough to see where the enemy came from. Abe was used to yelling directions: six o'clock, twelve o'clock … sometimes, only "*left!*"

If Cameron talked less, he would be able to see better, Abe kept telling him. Laughter followed. The mouth and eyes weren't connected, Cam said. They were, though. Everything was connected. Abe had learned that on the farm, as well as while fishing and hunting. Cameron should have, also. But the Terry farm had equipment, a lot of equipment. Cam knew how to run machines. He spent too much time letting the machines think for him.

"*Luchner.*"

He bolted at his First Sergeant's voice and stood at attention. He wished he'd left his boots on. Sand now coated the bottom of his feet.

"At ease."

Abraham lowered the salute and stood arms behind his back.

"If this were peace time, we would do this with more pomp. As it is, I'm here to add rank to your uniform." First Sergeant removed the pins on his collar and replaced them. "Congratulations, PFC Luchner. Few have raised rank so fast as a foot soldier."

"Thank you, First Sergeant." Abe remained in position until the tent flap closed again. He looked at the new pins. Private First Class. It wasn't much, he supposed, but it was another step up. His father would be proud.

"We'll be calling you First Sergeant before you know it." Cam slapped his back. "Congratulations Abe. Well deserved."

"Thank you. But I hope not to be out here long enough to go that far."

"You and me both, friend." Cam waved an envelope between them. "A new letter, nice and thick. How about celebrating with word from home?"

"I cannot think of a better way, unless it was to be sent home."

"Sent home already?" Cam curved one side of his mouth upward. "You are like a desert fish, Abe. You swim through this convoluted mess with the grace of a shark, as though you belong here. Do not tell me you are as tired of it as I am. I think I should be disappointed to hear if you are."

Abe brushed the sand off his feet as well as possible and leaned back on his bunk. "Being able to manage well does not mean I am content to stay. I will be more than glad to replace this sand and the jagged mountains with Idaho's sandy dirt and rounded soft mountains. And the gorge. The clear streams you can drink from. The smell of the animals. Tumbleweeds and rock chucks." He could see them in his mind. It was a sight that helped keep him going, a reminder of what he was there to protect. His farm. His piece of America. The right to work hard and earn his way and hold onto what he earned. To choose his wife and have children in numbers they could manage and raise them under their own beliefs, their own values. He had never known, before spending the past few months in this land, just how precious those things were.

They still dug wells by hand in this land, with few tools. There was little electricity and it was reserved for the very few wealthy, the government mainly, and those who worked for it. Scraps of leftovers were greedily accepted by children who tailed the soldiers whenever possible. Shoes without soles half gone were a luxury.

"Are you here?"

He looked over at Cam's waving hand. "Sorry. I suppose I'm rather tired tonight."

Cam laughed. "And what's different than any other night? Do you want to hear what Maura has to say?"

"If it is not an imposition. Nothing she wrote personally, of course. Only news of the town."

"She writes nothing so personal I cannot share it with you." Cam shrugged off a slight bitterness and kicked back, propped against his pillow, legs stretched out.

"*Dear Mr. Terry* ... no matter how often I have asked her to call me by my own name, she refuses to do so. Is that a bad sign?"

Abe shrugged. "You said she was raised a lady. Perhaps she is only following what she was taught, as you are not engaged yet."

"As though I need the reminder. Thank you." Cam cleared his throat and returned to the letter.

Dear Mr. Terry,

I fear my previous letter was not as long as you might wish, as I was grateful to finally hear from you and to know you were well and so, rushed through my response. I did not want you to wait long to see if I would reply as I said I would. The day I received your letter I was nearly too tired to hold my head up long enough to read it, and yet, I answered that night before allowing slumber.

I am glad, and relieved, you are well, and your friend, also. You must extend my appreciation for him looking after you, although it is my feeling you exaggerate. I am aware of how hard you work, of your aptitude, and am positive you would do well in any task you undertake. Now that I have embarrassed myself and perhaps moved beyond bounds I should not have crossed, let me turn my thoughts onto current news.

It is largely dreary news, I am afraid, for we receive more wounded on a too regular basis and I have extended my duties from taking care of babies and young mothers to assisting the nurses on the other side of the home. Currently, I am in the midst of reading Hemingway's 'Islands in the Stream' to those who cannot read themselves in their conditions. It was not my choice of books, although I enjoy the story. It deals with such loss and with a different war in a different time, and I am unsure it is entirely appropriate. They do appear absorbed in it, however. Possibly it is a cathartic experience. It is sad, do you not think, that the main character is such a grand artist and loses it for the different path he chose? Why, when one has a love and passion for what he does, would he cast it aside, particularly in the hardest times when it should comfort him, and heal him? I'm afraid I do not understand that part of the story, although he does do well in his new venture and provide a fitting service.

I should not assume, I suppose, that you have read the story and therefore follow my rambling. I am not sure whether you read much at all, other than the newspaper which I have seen you carry. As I write this, I think of so many things I have not yet learned about you. And you about me. I suppose there is time.

Perhaps our letters while you are away will be a quicker remedy.

And again, I overstep.

In town, not much has happened to relay. Fall is on the approach and there are whispers of snow in the mountains. Only the tops of the highest are tinged in white-grey as a warning more will come. Our farmers hope for a better snow this year, as I am sure you realize. We may get a few drops of rain tonight, which would be most welcome. The air does smell of it, but I withhold my hopes. It seems such a long time since I was able to sit on the porch and watch the rain drench the earth. I would appreciate the assistance, as I would not need, then, to water our garden in the morning. That sounds such a small thing to be concerned with to you, I have to think. You have greater worries about your days...

Tell me what your weather is like. How does the air feel and smell? Your letter contained a unique odor I cannot place and yet I cannot forget. What do you see as you look out around you?

As I walk out my door, I smell the voracious honeysuckle and the bright yellow and orange of the mums catch my eye. I must tell a rather embarrassing story on myself. Perhaps it will give you a laugh:

You do remember old Mrs. Marsh? She walks past each day up from her house to ours and back again. Although it's a matter of only four houses, she says it keeps her legs working and her heart pumping. I suppose that could be true, but with as many stories as are in her home, I have to think it would be enough to walk up and down them once or twice a day. She refuses to use a parasol, if you remember. Oh how I envy her that. Father would surely have a conniption if I walked about with my head uncovered and my face fully in the sun as I wish. I suppose it would not be wise. Here I am rambling again.

To get back to the story, a few days ago, I was bent down in my flower garden pulling weeds and I was so absorbed I failed to hear Mrs. Marsh walk up to the gate. I also failed to hear her speak to me until she came in the gate and touched my shoulder. The startle of it caused me to jump enough that I not only fell backwards into my asters, which fortunately seem to have survived, but also knocked poor Mrs. Marsh off balance enough she fell onto her ... let's suffice it to say I would have been largely embarrassed to have had to walk back the four houses with the back of my skirt marked so with dirt and grass stains. The dear lady stood there on our front lawn and brushed herself off, her backside and all, and laughed it off when I offered to get something to cover herself with on the way home.

She is a glorious woman, her chin straight, walking as though nothing happened after she allowed herself a laugh at her own expense. Well, I worried so much about what I had done to the lady that I lost track of my task and the time and rushed off to the home. It wasn't until I returned after quite a long day and changed into my house clothes that I noticed a larger and dirtier stain on the back of my skirt than Mrs. Marsh sported. I had worked all day and not one soul said a word.

My face began to redden there in the privacy of my room, and then I convulsed into laughter. It was indecent, I realize, and it is more indecent to tell you of it, I suppose. Do you wonder what they thought of my walking around that way? My chin was nearly as high as Mrs. Marsh's. They must have thought I had lost my sanity. I believe I was closer to doing so that evening while laughing than I have been for some time.

Perhaps I should not have repeated the story, but there is always a chance someone may mention to you that I was out in such a manner. I would rather you hear why I was from my own words. I would not want you to believe I have fallen into a disreputable state.

I am afraid my garden is becoming that, however. Father spends little time in it by now, as his frailty increases. I do worry for him, though he says he will stay around to see I am married and taken care of. I tell him I shall not marry for some many years ahead if that is what he waits on. He advises me not to linger.

As he spends less time tending the vegetables, I try to compensate. I enjoy it, as I believe you know. It may be quite the little scandal that I am too often seen with dirt on my fingers – I do detest wearing garden gloves even more than I detest the parasol – but it is honest work and refreshing to my soul. Still, the hours at the home have increased and I do not keep up well. I am afraid we will have to buy more vegetables from town this year. Father says I should let the garden go and buy them, as it will support those who live by selling their produce and will keep the dirt off my fingers. I believe he wishes for me to go and buy from your family as a means of entrenching myself in their presence. I'm afraid the idea is uncomfortable. Please accept my apology for saying so.

With that, dearest Mr. Terry, I shall need to end this letter and go out to tend the garden. I do not believe the rain will come and so I shall give it a good drink tonight before the sun sets fully. It is a magnificent orange-red sky tonight. I do so wish you could see it.

> *Be well, Cameron. I trust your return.*
> *Maura Laerty*

"She used your name."

Cam looked up with a light nod. "And she spoke of marriage. Do you think it could have been a suggestion that she awaits my proposal again?"

"I suggest you not think too hard on it." Abe took a lung-expanding breath and sat up, pulling his shower shoes onto his feet.

"Not think hard on it? And would you not be?"

"It is too much distraction. Your mind is better placed here where you are instead of home where she is. When you return, your marriage thoughts can return with you." Abe stood and reached high over his head to stretch his weary muscles. "I am off for a walk in the cool air and then a shower. If you return Miss Laerty's letter tonight, you may let her know my father always has extra vegetables on hand and will be glad to share."

Cam grinned. "Taking business from my parents?"

"You know that's untrue. I would hate for her to be uncomfortable about the arrangement, is all. Tell her, if you wish, that it would be in appreciation for allowing you to share her words of home. I can see it as she describes it. Your Miss Laerty has quite the poetic soul." Abe felt himself begin to flush. "Do not repeat that, only the offer. Perhaps she could relay news to my father in return." He didn't allow time for a response before he hurried out the tent flap and grabbed a lung full of cool desert air. The sky was morose compared to the picture Maura had just painted of her own. He decided to skip the walk and went straight to the shower.

six

Dearest Maura,

I've happy news to share. My friend Abe has just received another promotion. It means, of course, he has out stepped me again, but he well deserved the rank of PFC. He deserves higher, truth be told, but there is a rule that prevents skipping rank and one that says an amount of time that must be served in between. Although I am a big believer in exceptions, the Army is not.

He worries about rising too fast above me. I have told him not to think of it, but he is too full of humility. He doesn't see why the rest of us look to him as a guide even though he has no authority over us. I suppose that's untrue now, to an extent. A PFC is heading toward Corporal and does demand a certain amount of respect.

I am well. I won't tell you of the blisters on my feet since mine are no worse than any other of us. Or of the perpetual need for a warm shower and freshly laundered towel. Or of a morning to be allowed to lounge in bed late and stumble down to the kitchen to feast on warm rolls and fresh eggs and thick bacon. Or on a lovely face in the sunlight.

I must stop here. For your memory is too clear tonight and I am too tired and too far from home. Bless you for sending such a long, vivid letter. I read and reread it often, and often I read it again to Abe. I do hope you don't mind. His refuses to write his father or to allow me to write for him, as he feels it is for the best, and so does not receive word from home. Abe does seem to enjoy your words, however. He says you have a poet's soul, although I was not to tell you he said as much.

Be well, dear Maura. Remind those on the other side of the building that I'll return for you. And I aim well.

All my best,
Cameron

Maura set the letter on her lap and lay her head back against the chaise. A poet's soul.

She should write him, her Cameron. Her letters had fallen back to only twice a week and they took so long to get to him. This week she had only sent one.

Too much time was spent at the home and yet it seemed never

enough to help. The knowledge of how she provided comfort to those in need, which had previously staved off much fatigue, no longer dwelled within. She could see no difference. There was too much of it. Wives of the first wave of soldiers to go over were having waves of babies left behind. They came from many towns around, as the home was the only like it for miles. Many had family members to take them in until their men returned. Many did not.

Time she had at her father's home was too often now spent in care of him, handling things he could no longer handle and would not hire out. He wanted no other man in his house to care for it until he was not there. It was too prideful. Father was nearly eighty; no shame would come in accepting help from a younger man who could use the work. She sighed and lifted her head. No matter. She was strong and able, stronger than most of the girls in town, and more capable. She could at least be proud of that.

With another sigh, Maura pulled herself off the chaise and set the letter on the stand. She had to return downstairs and get dinner. Her father would also not hire a cook, and she didn't understand why he couldn't at least make that concession for her. He said he liked her cooking; it was like her mother's. What else would it be like since her mother had taught her? Maura could easily bring in a girl who needed work and teach her to cook the same. There were many who would accept, many who would be grateful.

He called out to her when she reached the bottom of the stairs. Casting her thoughts aside, she stepped into the library that had become his room. "I am about to start dinner, Papa. Do you need anything first?"

"Dinner can wait. Come sit with me." He held out a shaky, fragile hand.

She frowned as she took it. "Do you need the doctor?"

"Maura, dear. There is no point in a doctor now. Sit with me. It is time for you to know the details of running the house."

"Oh, but you're tired now and you'll be hungry soon. It can wait…"

"I am afraid it may not. Please, dear daughter, I will not rest well until I am reassured you will be all right. Take a pencil and pad and write my instructions. I should have brought you into them sooner, but I did so hope to wait until you were settled into a house of your own."

"And so you will. It is only a virus. You will be better in a day or two."

He patted the hand he held softly. "Let us hope that is true. If so, you will still be informed and I will still rest more easily."

Maura didn't have the heart to tire him with argument and went to the desk for the "miscellany" ledger her father used for notes and things to remember. She settled back into the wooden chair beside his bed and tried to grasp the important things from his rambles.

After a quick dinner of soft-cooked squash with extra butter, as her father insisted he had no further necessity to avoid whatever he wished to eat, and shredded pork roast, Maura tucked a blanket up around his shoulders and let him know she would be out for a few minutes while he napped. She couldn't stay out long, as the days were growing shorter and colder and it was close enough to scandalous for a young lady to walk along the streets alone. It wasn't quite, depending on how the lady was dressed and with whom she stopped to speak. After dark, however, she could be wearing four layers that made her look like a balloon and still be considered scandalous.

She pulled as much cool October air into her lungs as they could handle while she stepped off the porch. Pumpkins and jack-o-lanterns adorned steps and porches, none yet lit as they waited for All Hallowed Eve. A squirrel scampered away from one, taking a hunk of the lantern's mouth with it as it ran. Naughty squirrel. The child who carved the rather creative-looking face would be disappointed. Possibly, he wouldn't. Maura knew the child well. He was always racing up and down the sidewalks and drawing all over them with chalk. Many of the images could rival Picasso. A spirited boy, he was. She hoped his parents would be able to pivot that spirit to a creative, productive line of work.

It took her thoughts to Abraham, the wood carver. Had he been such a creative free spirit as a child? She now wished she had allowed Cameron to introduce them as he tried. She could never tell him why she would not. The glimpses she had of Abraham from a distance while he did chores in town made her fight a flush in her cheeks. It was highly embarrassing and disturbing. He moved nicely. He held his chin high enough but not too high. He spoke to nearly everyone and his manner showed he actually listened, with little return talk of himself as most did. Her father had caught her staring once. He pulled her right back home and let her know the Luchner boy was not in her stature and her eyes should remain elsewhere.

She especially could not have him come to her father's house with Cameron. Something was likely to be said, or she would be unable to resist the blush, and she did not want that kind of embarrassment. She never blushed with Cameron. Maura wasn't sure whether she should be glad she didn't or if it was a sign he was not the right one. The blush may have been embarrassing, but it stimulated her senses in a way Cameron never had.

"Good evening, Miss Laerty."

Maura startled at the voice at her side. "Oh, Mr. Weathers, how are you this evening?"

"I apologize for frightening you. Is everything all right? It is growing late."

"Yes, thank you. I only needed fresh air but I should turn back home now."

"I am going that way myself. Would you mind the company?"

"Not at all. To be honest, it would be a relief as I shall not have to hurry my steps to be in before dusk recedes."

Her gray-haired neighbor gave her a smile and offered his arm. As they strolled, he asked of her father and invited her for tea with his daughter. He spoke of how she was anxious to return to her own home when her husband returned. Her son's noise and commotion would be lost in the depth of the trees and acreage of their country estate. She worried he annoyed the neighborhood since he was used to running and shouting.

"Oh, he is a delightful child. Anyone who is bothered by him should simply make themselves less easily bothered."

Another smile highlighted the round face and friendly eyes. "Yes, it is a joy to have him about. Helps to keep me young."

"I am sure that is true." Sadness cast over Maura. She didn't believe her father would ever live to see his own grandchild since she had waited so long, and since her mother had trouble conceiving for so many years until they had expected to be childless. Perhaps a grandchild would have helped him remain younger, as well.

Mr. Weathers left her at her front porch with a nod and best wishes for her father and strolled back next door to his own house. Tony ran out to the porch to meet him. Maura did so wish her father could have that as well.

seven

Dear Cameron,

I apologize for my last letter being such a long time ago. Father was very ill and I needed the time to sit with him while he was awake and take care of the house matters while he slept. I am so very tired, although I should not complain considering what you have to deal with. My apologies again.

Maura set her pen down. She was too tired to write, although she knew she should. She didn't want to send complaints to Cameron to add to his worries. She wondered already if what she had written was too much a complaint. He would want to know that much, she supposed. It was hardly a complaint, if truth be told, compared to how much she had been through the past two weeks she wouldn't say. When her father was lucid, he fussed about how tired she looked, about how she wouldn't be presentable to her Mr. Terry when he came home for her. She tried to explain how much she was needed at the home, how at least she could help in this small way, and that she hoped someone would care as much for Cameron if needed.

She cringed at the thought and picked up the pen again.

Before I continue my letter to you, could you pass along a word to your friend? Miss Monroe is not looking well. She says, when I ask, that she has a lingering cold and will be well soon, but I believe she is suffering a broken heart, or at least an injured heart. She has not heard from her Mr. Luchner since he left. I am at a loss to understand, as all in town seem quite fond of him. I give her the news I hear from you and she was delighted to learn of his promotion. She would be more delighted, I believe, by a few simple words in a letter. Surely he can take a moment to do so.

Maura sighed and returned the pen to the desk, then ambled to her window. It was unfair, perhaps, to lay that on Cameron's shoulders. He did, however, throw Maura in the middle by asking her to pass the sketch along. Sadie seemed embarrassed when she received it. Maura vividly remembered the girl staring for the longest time before she mumbled quick thanks and hurried away. She missed Abraham dearly. Maura could read it in her face each time they met in town, before Sadie pulled her heavy cloak tighter and turned away from her. Maura took no offense. It was a rather common look on the faces of so many women and many chose avoidance, shopping as normal and acting as though nothing were wrong. They often shied from her gaze, as she was a caregiver, someone who reminded them of whatever care they'd received for whatever they could afford to pay. That was often nothing. It embarrassed them to no end.

How many more would there be? Four months had passed since Cameron and Abraham left. Many more had gone after them, some by choice, other by letter. In the past two weeks between caring for her father, Maura had helped with three deliveries by frightened young mothers, one a widow already, the others afraid they would be so. And the other end of the home continued to grow.

One of the newly wounded had taken an interest in her. He was a lovely man with dark brown eyes and a pretty smile. He didn't need much attention, intent to take care of himself as much as he could from the wheelchair he'd learned to spin in circles and race down hallways. Maura had told him, when he began to hint, of Cameron and his plea to tell others he would come back for her.

She had told herself she would never say so. She didn't care to be so attached in the minds of people in town. The young man was sure, though, her refusal was because of the wheelchair. Much of it was. She could never tell him so. He would never understand that she had enough to take care of without adding to it; that she wanted a partner she could work with side by side, a true partner, not needy and not controlling. She wasn't sure if Cameron would ever grow to be such. He had taken charge too much already by making his intentions too clear too soon and to too many. She was already betrothed to him, according to some of the whispers.

That bridge would need to be crossed as it approached.

And the letter to Cameron must be finished. She took another long glance out her window, over the distant field of hay, now mostly harvested, to her mountains. They reminded her of Abraham's sketch. She wished she'd kept it. It only seemed to upset Miss Monroe.

> *If you are thinking I have again overstepped my bounds*
> *with the suggestion above, you should know that each day I*
> *spend at the home and then in town with those I treat refusing*
> *my glance, I care less about bounds. There seem to be none in*

real life. Why, therefore, should we bother with them in proprieties? The ungentlemanly cads who spent their final days here with trusting girls and words of promise and lies of love should all be hung by their toes for what they have done. How will we ever recover in our proprieties with so much of it having been cast to the gorge due to 'celebration' or fear? It is high time we reconsider the important issues, that there are beautiful, sweet, caring young women who may not be quite as 'new' as men expect but who are only in that condition due to other careless, selfish men who left them in that state. It is high time for men to take responsibility for their own doings, their own reprehensible animal instincts that find it quite all right to sully certain young women and then desert them for those lucky enough to have avoided that fate. If they cannot keep other men from doing such, then they should be less particular and accept these women as they are, children and all. How else will we handle all of the young women with children and no means of their support?

Maura unclenched her jaw and breathed deeply, the scent of ink wafting into her nose. It was too blunt. She should burn it and start again.

She wouldn't, however. Cameron read the letters she wrote to Abraham. Perhaps it would be strong enough to make him at least send word to Miss Monroe. Refusing any contact, even if the rumors of their connection were as overstated as hers and Cameron's, was far too cruel. The girl wouldn't possibly be so upset if there wasn't something between them, something she counted on from him. She didn't seem the type to assume more than what had been stated. Sadie was, in fact, one of the few girls of her age group she would enjoy talking with.

Maura would try again. The next time she ran across Sadie, she would insist she come over for tea. She wrote as much as she continued the letter. Abraham should know. If there was anything he wished to hide, he would understand she meant to find it, to bring him out of hiding and be the responsible, valued gentleman the town treated him as.

eight

"What is it you're hiding?" Abe watched Cameron stuff something into the box under his bunk.

"Nothing of any concern."

"Not a new letter from Miss Laerty, then?" He threw a grin. Rarely a day passed his friend didn't mention her. Abe had grown used to it. He had grown to enjoy it, truth be told, although he would never say so.

"So tell me." Cam plopped on his bunk. "Why do you not write your father or any other soul?"

"I told you why."

"So he doesn't worry if the letters pause too long or stop. But Abe, don't you think he'd at least get enjoyment when they do come?"

"He knows I am well if he hears nothing. They read lists of injured and dead in town. He will know if I am not. I won't have him wondering every day if there will be a new letter. It seems cruel."

"So you think I am cruel writing to Maura?"

Abraham shoved his boots from his feet and leaned back on his bunk.

"You won't answer?"

"You don't want my answer."

Cameron came over and sat next to him. "I do. Say so."

"I think it's cruel to continue to promise you will return whole and healthy when you do not know you will. I made no such promise to anyone. My father will adjust while I am away and if I do not return, it will not be a shock to have to change his thoughts."

"But writing letters would not…"

"I don't wish to discuss it."

"You don't think you'll return."

Abe grabbed the folder of blank paper and stick of charcoal from his stand, and shut Cameron's question out of his mind. He used the unkempt sketching to distract him from the day's events, with images of the landscape around him, brief glimpses he caught of something that stood out away from why he was there, or sometimes pictures from memory of home or a scene from his travel. Each day he erased by slipping elsewhere on fresh paper. Each new day, he started again and made sure to find at least one thing he could incorporate into his sketches.

He wouldn't abandon his creative urge as Hemingway's hero had. Perhaps his own story would turn out the better for it.

+_+_+

Maura threw on a grin, as well as she could manage, and welcomed Miss Monroe. She hadn't expected the girl to show at her front door. She could not, however, turn her away. She looked worse than she had a few days before when they ran across each other in town.

"Would you like a cup of tea?"

"Oh, thank you." Sadie glanced around the parlor as though she expected someone else to enter. "I don't wish to be a bother. Thank you for allowing me in. I shouldn't have come."

"I rarely have company. I'm glad to have you, although I am unsure why I have the pleasure of the visit." Maura led her to a chair. "Let me take your wrap."

"Oh, no, I'll keep it on." Sadie lowered into a chair, using her arms to hold part of her weight.

"Do you feel well?" Maura sat across from her. Then she stood again. "Please, let me get us refreshments. I baked banana bread earlier. Father will not eat it so I would be glad to have company. I'll be back in a moment." She didn't allow Sadie to object. The girl looked to need food. And refreshment.

On return, she set the dish and tea cup on the table at Sadie's side and went to retrieve her own.

"I am very grateful." Sadie took a nice, healthy bite of the bread and washed it down with tea.

"You haven't yet told me why you came by tonight."

"No." She took another swallow, not a delicate sip as Maura had been taught, but a nice, hearty swallow. "My apologies. I find it hard to discuss."

"Are you well, Miss Monroe?"

"Sadie. Please, call me Sadie. I'm afraid I wasn't brought up so formally. I do try. Mama despairs that I try to act the proper lady when we are, as she says, normal working people, and I should not try to be other than that. It's misleading and dishonest, she says."

"I cannot see being proper as a requirement for only one ... well, I see no harm in manners." Maura was careful with her phrasing. To insult Sadie's mother would not be at all proper.

"I'm afraid it's harder for some of us to do. Even if we mean well." She swallowed more bread. "I did try. I ... I did the unspeakable and ... and fell for a lovely, proper man. He didn't pay much notice of me. I suppose he could see I wasn't enough of his class. Although ... Mama says he's not one of the proper gentlemen of town even if he acts as though he is."

"Abraham." Maura startled herself saying his first name aloud. She shouldn't have.

Sadie was startled, as well. "Yes. I am afraid I made a fool of myself because of him." She tilted her head at Maura. "You know him, then?"

"No." Maura straightened her shoulders. "I have seen him in town. When he was still in town. We haven't met. I mainly know of him through Camer... through Mr. Terry."

Sadie pulled her eyes away and swallowed tea. "Yes. Mr. Terry." She raised them again. "Do you love him the way I love my Abraham?"

"Oh." The question made her nearly drop her cup.

"I'm sorry. That was inappropriate. However ... it is something I would like to know. You see, I..."

"You would like to know if what those in town say is true?"

"Yes."

"We are not betrothed."

"No?"

"No."

"I have heard often...." She pulled her eyes again.

"People have presumed too much, I'm afraid."

"Then, you have no intention of becoming betrothed to Mr. Terry?"

Maura took a moment to compose an answer. "I do not wish to settle my future when I see no reason to rely on it as of yet."

Her mouth gaped. "You do not trust him to return to you? I mean ... as in keeping his word to want you as a wife when he is home again."

"I'm afraid that is not my concern. It would be much simpler if it were." Maura stood and took Sadie's empty plate and cup. She went into the kitchen, refilled both, and handed them to the girl.

"Oh, please, I've taken enough of your hospitality."

"No, I'm glad you are here to share." Maura sat again, fully uncomfortable. "Why is it that you came to me tonight?"

Sadie threw her a sad grin. "I'm in need of assistance. I had hoped we could get to know each other more before I asked. Although I have no right to ask. And I should not be here. There is no one else. And I cannot..." She ducked her head behind a hand.

"Sadie?" Maura went to her and touched her forehead. "I am not a nurse. If you need medical care you should come to the home in the morning and..."

"I am with child."

Maura stepped backward. Another one. Unmarried. She wanted to flee to her room and hide behind her door. So much for Abraham Luchner being a gentleman and honorable as Cameron always stated.

"Mama says I am not to stay at home with her. I must marry the boy who did this and stay with him as is meant to be."

"She doesn't know he's away?"

Sadie shook her head. "I have not told her who the father is. And I cannot. I cannot tell anyone. It would cause too much harm to too many."

"It is his responsibility." Maura threw her shoulders back. "If he was worried about his reputation, he should have thought of that before..."

"No." Sadie caught her eyes. She looked tired, more tired than Maura, and fearful, and sad. "Do not blame him. I ... I was responsible. I was angry and hurt and ... I should not have encouraged him."

"Still. A gentleman, even if encouraged, has the duty to be responsible..."

"Miss Laerty..."

"Maura. Please. If we are to share this intimacy, you must use my first name."

She gave her another sad grin. "Then you will help? I realize the home is closed now but I have nowhere to go. Could you have someone let me in tonight? I don't wish to be on the street, for the sake of my child..."

"You'll stay here."

Sadie's eyes widened. "Oh, I couldn't. I'll soil your reputation and I've already done enough..."

"You certainly won't. The townsfolk know how I help at the home. They know we are overflowing. They'll think nothing of my offer to allow you to stay. And I insist. Please, finish your bread and tea and I'll go and prepare a room." Without time for response,

Maura hurried away.

Her father would be furious, she supposed, but he would have to manage to be polite, as a gentleman would be to any lady. Even an unmarried lady expecting a child she had no means to care for.

nine

Maura was content to leave Sadie to watch over her father as she walked to town, with basket on her arm. She had left her Thanksgiving dinner shopping go far too long and hoped there was still a decent selection of fresh turkeys and yams and cranberries. Her pumpkin was already safely nestled on her porch; it served as fall decoration until she would pull it in to make pie.

"Good morning, Miss Laerty."

She gave a light grin to the friendly voice. "Good morning, Mr. Weathers. How are you today?"

"Well, thank you. Susanna has the house full of heavenly smells: apples, cinnamon, pumpkin. I would suppose yours is the same by now?"

"I'm afraid I'm behind this year. I'm just on my way to find what is left to throw together."

Mr. Weathers stepped out from his yard and joined Maura on the sidewalk. "My dear, you and your father are welcome to join us, if you'd like. You have your hands much too full."

"Oh, thank you. I wouldn't dream of imposing. You do have relatives coming in again, I hear. Your house and hands will be quite full enough."

"Two more should make no difference."

"Three might." Maura watched for the condescending look that had started around town since Sadie moved in.

"I thought Miss Monroe would be home for Thanksgiving, as she should. Is she not?"

"Her mother will not allow her in the house until she marries the father, which she cannot do at the present moment." Maura felt a light blush. "I will understand if you feel the need to disassociate from us as long as she stays. I will not, however, kick her out with nowhere to go."

"My dear, I will do no such thing. You may bring Miss Monroe, if you wish. Let them say anything to me about it."

Maura was highly tempted to accept. She didn't wish to cook, to spend so much of her little energy all day in the kitchen first cooking then cleaning. However, the offer was far too generous. She saw no point in adding one more in town to the firing line. "Thank you again, but I'm afraid Father will be much too stubborn to go elsewhere for Thanksgiving. He'll want to stay in as always."

Mr. Weathers gave her a soft understanding bow and offered an arm. "Then at least allow me the pleasure of your company as I am heading the same direction."

She dropped her groceries onto the kitchen counter and stored the scrawny turkey in the icebox until morning. Maura frowned again at the berries that were not quite fresh but the best she could find, the few yams left after being picked through by the rest of the town, and a few other mixings that would have to do.

She'd run into Mrs. Terry and her sons. They'd hired some young boy to carry their shopping baskets, never mind he was as scrawny as the turkey she'd found and the Terry boys were well built and quite able to carry their own. Maura had been weighed down by her own basket. Mrs. Terry threw a deprecating grin, tossed her chin, and asked of her father. Maura knew she had no real interest and only spoke to her because others were around and had connected Maura to her eldest son. She offered assistance, as well. Maura said she needed none. The offer was loud, for the benefit of passersby. The following comment about *that* girl staying in her house not being fit for Cameron's suitor was quiet. And pointed.

Maura very much wanted to say they should look down at Cameron's friend, not at her; she didn't get the girl into the mess. Instead, she raised her own chin, assured her Cameron knew Sadie stayed at her place and didn't seem at all concerned, and walked past.

The truth was Maura had no idea what Cameron thought of Sadie staying there. She hadn't heard from him since her last letter, nearly a month before. Possibly the mail had slowed again. Possibly she'd been far too outspoken.

With a sigh, she went to check on her father and nearly ran into Sadie outside his door.

"I thought I heard you come in. Did you find everything you needed?"

"Enough that will do. How is he this morning?"

"Cranky as ever." Sadie grinned. "He asked why it didn't smell of pumpkin in the house yet."

"I should tell him if he doesn't stop being cranky, it won't, either."

"Yes, I'm sure you'll tell him that." Sadie's smile was at least half cheery by this point. "I have some errands of my own to run. Do

you mind if I go quickly? I'll return to help with the cooking. I won't
be long."

"You don't need to ask permission. I am grateful for your help
as I have it, but I do not require it as a condition to stay. You first
need to care for yourself and your child."

"You are much too good to me, and to everyone else." Sadie
stepped closer. "Maura, please remember you should, at least at
times, put yourself first." Then she withdrew toward the hall. "I
won't be long. Wait until I'm back and we'll cook together."

+_+_+

Dearest Cameron,

*It has been the longest time since I've heard from you. There
has been no news to report from the front, so I have to believe you
are well and simply tired. I will continue to write, as you asked,
until I hear something of you either way. Did that sound
dreadful? I did not mean it that way. I worry, you realize, but I
know you are able and strong and will take care of yourself. Please
remember your vow to oblige my request that you return standing.*

*We had a lovely Thanksgiving, larger than I expected since
Miss Monroe is still here with us and I quite enjoy the
companionship. She was out on errands the afternoon before and
brought a boy back with her. Do not concern yourself. He is only
seven or eight, as I can tell. He seems unsure of his age. His name
is Rudy. A pleasant lad, he is horribly malnourished, and said he
was brought to town by a relative he was stuck with who drove on
without him. They traveled quite some distance to get here. It
appears to be intentional abandonment. He has been managing on
his own for some time, but Sadie insisted he come for the holiday. I
have offered him a safe place to sleep in exchange for help with
house and yard chores. Father tried to refuse. I am embarrassed to
say I overruled his objection. As he is no longer able to help even
with the lightest chores, I do believe I have the right to hire who I
need, and a boy who will work for room and board is barely hired.*

*He is quite attached to Sadie already. She has such a kind
heart and nurturing hands and enjoys having him to pamper as
he'll allow. He never allows her out without being her chaperone,
so he says. I hope, by this time, the relative does not bother to
return, as both Rudy and Sadie are flourishing with the mutual
care I have little spare time for. Even my father is taking well to
Sadie, despite his best intent not to do so.*

I'm afraid I must make this a short letter. Although I should hardly apologize since I have written you several that have not been answered.

I do hope you are well. I will not complain about a two sentence letter if that's all the energy you can muster. Please let me have just a word to know you have not forsaken my friendship only because of my pertinence of that letter you should burn. I do so count on ... if not more than that, at least your continued friendship.

Yours,
Maura

As she sealed the letter, Maura gulped a deep breath and held it until the mistiness in her eyes stopped. She needed fresh air, despite the cold. Early December and the winds already bit at times as they blew down from the mountains. There was time left to walk to the mail and back before dusk. She paused only long enough to tell Sadie where she was headed and refused Rudy's offer to mail it for her.

Maura walked briskly as the wind slapped at her cheeks underneath the heavy bonnet and scarf. Perhaps she shouldn't mail it. Did it sound too urgent? Too needy? She'd only asked for his friendship, nothing more, although more than friendship did cross her mind more often each day. The way he held her against his strong body when she hugged him that last day echoed through her memory. The fit of his arms around her back had given her such a sense of safety, of a possibility of someone to care for her instead of the other way around. He wanted to take care of her. Maura knew he did. By this time, a small part of her wondered if she should accept. It was harder each day to make herself go to the home. There was too much need there. Too much they wanted her to give.

A sting at the corner of her eyes made her realize she was allowing her emotions to show. She bit her lip hard to stop it. It burned; a combination of cold and dry accented the sharpness of her teeth.

No one spoke to her either on her way to or from. She didn't mind. Maura had no interest in gossip or their condescending looks and hints. She pulled the door shut and pulled the cold outer garments off, in search of the warmth inside the house.

"Maura!"

She jumped at Sadie's cry and turned to find her friend hurrying forward, an arm supporting her abdomen. "What is it? Are you ill? Is it the baby?"

"No, your father. I was about to send Rudy to find you."

Father. Maura rushed to his room. He gasped for air. She half turned to Sadie. "Send Rudy for a doctor. Tell him to hurry." Pulling the chair up to her father's bed, she stroked his head. "It's all right, Papa. We're fetching the doctor. Try to relax."

"A wasted effort." He choked out the words. "Maura, my ... my beautiful girl. This ... is all ... yours now. You take care of it and be sure... be sure to protect ... protect it."

"Don't talk now. Rest. Wait for the doctor."

"I am sorry. I ... hoped to wait ... until your Mr. Terry returned ... did not want ... to leave it all on you. You rest. Be wary." His eyes closed.

"Papa. Don't leave me now. Please." Maura took his hand and raised it to her cheek. "Not now. I need you here. I can't do all this alone, with Sadie and the little one coming and the children and the soldiers. More every day, Papa. I need you to stay."

"You will be fine, Maura dear." He gasped air into his lungs, a pained expression on his face. "There is money enough in the account..."

"I am not concerned about the money. I need you here."

"No, I have ... been one more thing ... for you to take care of. It ... has not been fair. Your mother. Then me. And all those boys. Be wary of them." He gasped harder, coughed, settled. "Marry the one you will be happy with, not the one you think you should." He bent with the cough this time.

"Papa..."

"Listen. Your mother ... should have married better. Not for ... security as she did, but ... for love as she should have ... should have had. I did love her. I fear ... I could not ... make her love me. Do not do the same, my Maura. You deserve better. As your mother did."

Maura was shocked by his words. She never would have thought her mother did not want to be married to her father. She never showed it. But she rarely smiled. She was sick too often.

Tears welled and she pushed them back. She couldn't use the energy for something so childish.

Her father's eyes closed. His breathing became shallow, raspy.

"Papa." Her voice was no more than a whisper. "Papa, please. Do not leave me now. Please."

"Maura?"

She turned at Sadie's voice.

"I am sorry..."

"He is alive. Did you send Rudy?"

"I did and he ran all the way there and back, but..."

"Where is he, then? There isn't time to spare."

Sadie shook her head. "There are more wounded just in. No doctors are available. Can we do something?"

Her mouth gaped. None available? None *available*? After the endless hours she put in helping others, of her own time, as she asked nothing? None were available to come to her assistance?

"Maura..."

She turned to her father's face.

"Do not worry. They cannot put a sick old man's life in front of a young man's. The young men are needed, as many as ... we can save. You are right ... in what you do. I am proud ... you are my daughter." He managed a slight grin. "Be well, my Maura. Protect yourself. Follow your heart. It has done you well." He closed his eyes, the breathing slowed.

"Papa?" There was no response. "Please." She looked up toward the ceiling. Beyond. "Please. Don't leave me to be alone. Please."

"You are not." Sadie came up behind her and touched her back. "I am here with you."

Maura shook her head. She needed more. She needed her father. Or for Cameron to return. She would even accept his hand if he would only return. Her strength was too far gone. Sadie was six months along. She would need.... Her father's chest stopped rising. He carried a peaceful expression. "Papa?" She felt for breath and found none. "No."

Sadie wrapped arms around her as well as she could. "You aren't alone. You helped me when I needed you. I will always be here at your service."

Maura couldn't allow the words in. She wouldn't allow the tears. She was alone. The last of her family. It all belonged to her now. The responsibility of being the last.

+_+_+   Winter   +_+_+

ten

"She's alone."

Abe pushed himself up to sitting . "What?"

"Maura. Her father died. She's alone now." Cameron stood and slipped into his boots, dropping the letter on his bunk.

"Where are you going?"

"To the lieutenant. I must return home."

Abe jumped to stop him. "You cannot."

"Abe, she is alone."

"Is there no one who will help? She has money, then, doesn't she? Relatives? Friends?"

"She has no family. The town fills with more soldiers daily. Many are recovering. Do you think she will remain safe there alone?"

Abraham tried to argue. They would never let Cameron leave because a girl who wasn't even his fiancée lost her father. He almost couldn't argue. He didn't want her alone, either. "What of your family? Will they not take her in as your intended?"

Cameron turned away.

"Cam? What is it?"

His friend sank to his bunk and dropped his head onto his hands. Abe went to sit next to him. "Have you done something to anger your father again?"

A nod answered.

"Still, he wouldn't hold it against her."

A huge breath raised Cameron's shoulders and dropped them again. "I've done something terrible, Abe. I'll have to tell you now but I am not sure I can make myself admit it."

"You have admitted plenty to me already, my friend, and I still call you friend. What is it? Get it off your chest."

He was silent for some time. Then he handed Abe the letter. "Read it. I can't admit it. You'll have to read it."

"The letter is to you, not to me." Abe accepted with a deep longing to keep it in his hands, to see if there was a hint of a smell to it the way Maura often tried to describe the smell of letters Cameron sent to her. He didn't dare. It was not to him.

"Please, Abe. Read it. Over there. At your own bunk. I'll need warning to fend for myself when you do."

Abe laughed. "Fend for yourself? You think I don't get enough fighting…?"

Cameron fell down into his pillow.

Letter in hand, Abe obeyed and took it to his bunk. As he settled, he couldn't resist a quick sniff. He wished he hadn't. It smelled of home, of … of a woman. It smelled of Maura, at least as he figured. Pushing the thought from his head, he leaned back against the pillow and opened the pages.

Dearest Cameron,

I have such news to share with you and I have gone through too many sheets of linen while trying to write it. However this comes out, I will have to send it. My strength doesn't permit another attempt.

I have tried so to spare you any sad or unhappy news and share only the beauty of home, of hope that still pervades the air, although it is becoming harder to find. Many of the wounded are on their way to recovery and often laugh while playing cards or throwing horseshoes or flirting with those of us who care for them. Do not worry for me. It is harmless. They only need a distraction. I have, as you asked, mentioned you enough they know their flirtatiousness will not sink in. And they know your family is close to town and would defend your honor. All is well on that front.

In other news, Father has passed finally. He is at peace now and watching over me from above, along with Mama. I do hope they are happy together, although from what Father confessed … I should not be writing this but I must talk and I have no one else in whom I can confide. I am sorry. You may skip ahead if you wish…

Papa beseeched me before he left to take care of my heart and honor it. With very heavy heart, I fear he read my true feelings. I am not sure … maybe you are not reading this and my words will have no effect. It would be better that way. I must tell you, as I can no longer be dishonest with you, that I am unsure we are meant to be a couple. I may be wrong. It may be when this is all over and you return that my feelings will be different. I am so tired. I am home today to write this because I was sent away. My father's funeral was a hard process to attend to, with everyone's minds on those still needing care. I did manage to handle it all and you would be proud as I never once allowed tears to interfere with what must be done. I have never been fully sure of my strength until now. But you would be proud … and as I worry about you being proud, I must think my feelings are mistaken.

I no longer realize just what I am writing and should burn this on the fire as well as the others. Perhaps I will.

There now, that frees me to write what I need to say. Then I can think of it further with a clearer head.

We will see, when you return, how we both react. I know it is possible you have changed while away. I know I have. I am unsure if I have made you any promises, as everything from before is now a blur. If I have and if you remember, I am sure you will want what is best for us both.

Oh dear, I ramble away again. I do not know my own thoughts. I know I am happy to have given you the answer I did before you left, although I cannot be sure you do not harbor some anger toward me for it.

Dear Cameron, my dear Cameron. Let me move on to other things now, more important things, as possibly none of what I said will matter.

I do hope your friend Abraham is well. I hope this because he is your friend only. Otherwise I should think the worst of him.

Abraham sat up. "Think the worst of me? Whatever for?" He looked over at Cam, who lay on his bunk with an arm across his face.

"Keep reading."

With a frown, Abe settled back in to find where he left off.

Have you passed along my messages to him? If you have not, then I shall be angry with you. If you have, I will have a very hard time finding an excuse no matter how well you speak of him. Sadie is so very much in need of a letter. Only a quick note. She refuses to write him unless he write first. There is something he must know, however, and I fear he will never write. I may cross bounds bigger than the Snake River Canyon by passing this along, but I feel I must. Sadie is with child. As I write, she is six months along and not feeling well…

With child? Abraham tore his eyes from the letter. She married after he left? Six months? She would have had to marry within days after he left. He made the right choice then, to discourage her. But what did it have to do with him? He went back to reading.

I worry for her health. Rudy follows her around to help as he can. She has taken him in nearly as a mother and has promised she will be that to him. He is old enough only to be of some help with chopping wood and doing chores I am too tired for and Sadie is restricted from. He is a sweet boy and a joy to have around. I find myself enjoying his company and thinking of … and I am off track again.

Sadie is much too tired for only being as far as she is. I believe it is fear – fear of being a single mother no man will accept because she is unmarried. If your friend Abraham is as much a gentleman as you say, he will do the right thing and at least send her a promise of marriage…

"What?" He jumped out of bed and headed to Cameron, noting his friend didn't bother to defend himself. He kept his arm over his face. "Why does she think I should marry Miss Monroe when she is expecting some man's child? Cameron?"

"Keep reading."

Abe nearly shoved his friend onto the floor. But he supposed he would finish the letter first.

This way the townspeople will not look so far down on her and she will feel more secure and I'm sure her health would improve. Please pass this along to Mr. Luchner and see if he has no feeling at all for the woman he took advantage of before he left…

"I did no such thing! Why would she think so? If Miss Monroe is telling the town I am the father … why would she? I was never rude to her. I never … I never so much as touched her more than offering my arm as we walked."

"I know you didn't. It hurt her feelings that you didn't. She wanted to marry you, you do know."

"But I never…. We talked at times. She was a lovely girl. I told her I wanted no attachment before I left. Why would she ruin my reputation…?"

"She hasn't told anyone."

"Hasn't told anyone? Then what is this letter about?"

"She only mentioned to Maura how she missed you. Maura presumed it was you since you were all she talked about."

"But … how do you know this?"

Cameron sighed and sat up. "It was in the other letter. The one I didn't read to you."

Abraham stared. "Other letter? You knew she claimed me as

the father and you didn't tell me? How could you…?"

"I didn't know she was expecting until just now. Maura asked me to push you to write Sadie because she was heartbroken. I couldn't do it."

"Heartbroken? If she was, it wasn't over me. It hardly took her more than a few minutes after I had gone to find another."

Cameron raised his eyes. "You do have feelings for her."

"I most certainly do not. She is a liar. And she is … she is…"

"You cannot say it. You do have feelings that keep you from saying it."

"I did have." Abraham hated to admit it, and he never would to anyone but his friend. "Yes. I did have. If I returned, I would have asked to see her. I am glad now I did not. What a fool I was. What a laughingstock she would have made me. Are you sure she has told no one this? If my father was to hear…"

"No one. Maura says she will not discuss it." Cameron dropped his head back onto his hands.

Abe studied him. Why did it bother him so? Why… why was he afraid of Abe's reaction, of needing to defend himself?

"Why?" He shuffled closer. "Why did you hide it from me?"

"I didn't want to lose Maura."

"But what does that have to do…?"

"The child is mine, Abe. Did I have to say it? You couldn't figure it out, as smart as you are? It's mine. I was with her the night before we left, after you turned her away and she was upset and after Maura turned me away and I was upset. We found each other and neither of us intended it. She stayed with me that night. In a barn with horses overlooking and…"

Abe walked away, out of the tent into the dark night and cold air. He had to walk away. Otherwise, he would attack his friend and he was tired of fighting, of attacking. It settled nothing. There were always more to fight, to attack. They wouldn't stop. They knew they were defeated and they wouldn't stop coming. Why wouldn't they just stop? It was only a matter of time. They knew it. Everyone knew it. Why keep going?

He gulped cold, sandy air and wished desperately to be back on his farm looking out at his mountains. Had his father heard? He would be disappointed if he had. Abe would have to write to him. But what if he hadn't? Then he would be telling Cameron's secret for no reason.

For no reason. There was a reason. And it could not stay a

secret.

He rubbed his hands together and went back into the tent, to where Cam still slumped on his bunk. "Propose to her."

The tired eyes met his.

"You propose to her. You write her and tell her you will marry her upon your return. I will never forgive you unless you do. I will not call you my friend again unless you do. You make this right, as right as you can."

"I'll lose Maura."

"You don't deserve her." Abe heard it leave his mouth but couldn't stop it. Still, it was true.

+_+_+

"What did you tell her?" Abraham gave him a look from overtop the Humvee. "I saw you mail out a letter. What did you say?"

Cam pushed his helmet up part way to scratch his head. "I told her you were not the father."

Abe waited for more. No more came. "While I appreciate that, there is much more to say. I hope you did." He ducked at a loud noise and swiveled to see an empty barrel rolling from where it dropped. "You did tell her."

"I sent along a note for Sadie."

"Good. What did you tell her?"

"I said I would take responsibility, and I added money to it with promise of more. I'll write my family tonight to let them know and to offer assistance until I return." Cam shrugged. "Satisfied?"

Abraham figured he should be. Those were the most important issues. Still, something niggled in his brain. "And Maura? What did you tell her?"

"I believe that's between the two of us."

Cam was right. It was. Except it was wrong to cheat on a woman and not admit it. It was wrong to cheat on her. She deserved better. She worked hard to help others as she could, tiring herself too often. And now she was without her father and with care of Sadie.

Abe pulled open his door when the captain yelled and jumped behind the wheel. Cam took his side, as always. As the convoy headed toward their destination, Abe couldn't help say more. "You think she will not find out if your family knows? Everyone will know. It would be better from you."

"I'll lose her."

"I would say it's too late for that. You lost her when you decided to be with Sadie. Be glad enough you haven't lost our friendship, as well. Although I did consider it." Abe swerved around a deep pit in the road. "Besides, it seems she was unsure. Add that to you being away for months longer, maybe years, and there wasn't much chance of holding onto her."

eleven

Maura refused to cry. She didn't want him, anyway. She'd decided, since she sent the letter, that it wouldn't work. Her feelings weren't strong enough. Her heart led her away. Still, for him to have done such a thing – not only to her but to Sadie, as well – was unforgiveable. Cameron knew how Maura felt about men who did such things, who left women they treated as disposable with no way out but poverty and helplessness. He knew. And he did it. While he was courting *her*, not to mention.

She held her chin up and shoulders back and took the letter over to the fireplace. With hardly a glance, she tossed it in.

Well, that was done. Nothing changed. She was still on her own with Sadie and young Rudy and they were doing fine. Maybe Sadie could at least start to feel better. Cameron said he sent money and would support her, would ask his family to look out for her and for his child. She would be well cared for. Maybe she would even move in with his family. Not if Maura could get her to stay. She needed the company.

With one last sniff as though daring her tears, she crept down the stairs and to the kitchen. Rudy was storing the groceries she'd sent him to fetch. They would have a nice big supper and celebrate: her freedom and Sadie's engagement. Cameron said he would marry her upon his return, to fulfill his obligation. At least he was man enough to do that much.

Maura didn't want him, anyway. He was too childish. Too … too irresponsible. Not what she needed.

She would write to Abraham and apologize. It was her responsibility to do so after the horrible thing she assumed of him.

"The tomatoes are nice and fresh today, Miss Maura." Rudy grinned as he showed her. "I got them straight from old Mr. Jakes's greenhouse. Look how beautiful they are."

She couldn't help but return his smile. He was such a sweet boy, one who cared about the quality of good vegetables and fruits. "Yes." She took it in her hand and felt its ripe plumpness. "It is beautiful indeed. You are such a wonderful treasure, Rudy. I don't know how I can thank you."

"Oh Miss Maura, no need to thank me. I don't have to sleep in alleys and in barns where I'm chased out anymore. That's enough.

And I get nice, fresh tomatoes from time to time." He grinned again.

"You get all the fresh tomatoes for us you like. They'll help you stay strong and healthy." Maura rubbed his brown hair.

"I hope they will help Miss Sadie get more healthy, too. She always looks so sad. Because she doesn't feel well, she says. Do you think the tomatoes will help?"

"Yes. I think they might. Run along and get cleaned up now and I'll make us something nice to go with these." She watched the boy scamper away. He worried so about Sadie. Of course, she had made herself his mother, by all rights. He would have reason to be concerned if anything were to happen.

Which it wouldn't. Cameron knew now. He would support her now. All would be well.

Stuffed full of meatloaf and potatoes and bread and nice, ripe tomatoes, Maura trudged up the stairs to her room. Since she had cooked, Sadie and Rudy were cleaning up. And she was tired.

She nearly laughed at the thought. She didn't remember anymore not being tired. It was part of life, just as having more injured and sick and lame than healthy and uninjured was now part of life. Pulling out of her gown, Maura filled the tub halfway with warm water and slipped out of the rest of her things. A long hot soak would revive her.

Except as she sat there, she thought of Cameron's words: how he missed warm baths and fresh towels. Her eyes moistened. She had no right to complain about how tired she was considering what the boys were going through in defense of her freedom – of her country's, but that included her. When she wrote to Abraham, she would write Cameron, also.

She stayed in the tub until the water cooled enough to chill her. She dried and dressed quickly. Maura couldn't even enjoy the luxurious feeling of her thick, soft robe. It made her think of scratchy green thin blankets and stiff uniforms packed with sand in each crevice.

Trying to push it from her mind, she sat at her writing desk and began a letter … to whom first? She held the pen in her hand and wondered. Cameron, of course. He should be first.

But Cameron's letter would be harder. She started with Abraham.

+ + +

"It's for you."

Abe untied his boots and raised his eyes to Cam. "What is?"

"A letter."

"I don't get letters. I don't write any and so I don't get any."

"You got one today." Cameron tilted his head. "I almost thought about not giving it to you, or at least reading it first. It's from Maura."

Abe forgot his laces and sat up straight. "Maura? But why?"

Cam shrugged. "That's what I wonder. You haven't written her behind my back?"

"I would never. You know I would never. I don't even write my own father. Why would I write your beloved?"

"So take it. And tell me what she says."

Abraham studied the letter in Cameron's fingers as though it was a bomb waiting to explode. Why would Maura write him? When he didn't accept, Cameron tossed it on his bunk and strode away. Insulted. But there was no reason for him to be insulted by or angry with Abe. He'd done nothing.

With a glance at it, he leaned down to finish untying his boots. The letter would wait. He wanted to get as clean as he could manage first.

He shivered as he quickly scrubbed himself under the makeshift shower tent that provided only cold water, non potable at that. It didn't block his thoughts from the letter on his bunk. Maybe Cam would give in to his curiosity and read it first. It would be better if he did. Abe was sure it was nothing. Or maybe it was news of his father.

The idea quickened his pulse and he decided he was clean enough. And cold enough. He was always cold enough now. As he dried, he thought back to his lieutenant's warning of how they would miss the sweat running down their foreheads and backs once winter came. Abe supposed that was very soon to be true. It wasn't yet. Even cold too often, it was at least cleaner than dripping sweat and attracting gnats and sand flies.

He didn't look over at Cam as he pushed beneath his thin green blanket. A fleeting thought of the thick blanket on his bed at home invaded: denim squares from worn pairs of blue jeans sewn together by his grandmother when he was a boy and soft fleece on the underside against his skin. He could almost believe he was covered by it now as he picked up Maura's letter. It was still where

Cam had tossed it. Unopened.

Careful to tear only the top edge, Abe nearly shook as he pulled the letter out. It must be word of his father. But she could have written that to Cam and had him pass it along.

He grabbed a deep breath, ignored the stare from his friend, and opened the pages. Page. Only one.

Dear Mr. Luchner,

I am afraid I must apologize deeply to you for the insinuating remarks in my last letter to Mr. Terry. I was of the belief you and Sadie – Miss Monroe – were better acquainted. She talked of you so, I could hardly think otherwise. It was my error and I do hope you will forgive my pertinence.

This is a rather embarrassing situation for me so it is good I will have time to recover from my error before we meet, as I feel we will in time. Sadie stays with me. I am sure Cameron – Mr. Terry – has told you. We have become close enough I will hope to stay in touch with her once she finds a better place to be, with her husband.

I shall miss her company. I realize it may be embarrassing to you, as well, to have to meet me, but I don't see how it can be avoided due to my friendship with Sadie and yours with Mr. Terry.

With all proper respect, I shall not again mention this and pray you won't either, when we do run across each other.

Thank you for understanding. Thank you, also, for looking after Cameron, as well, as he says you do. Sadie will be much happier when she can be with the father of her child as she should be.

With all respect,
Maura Laerty

Abraham stared a moment. She'd signed it with her first name, not with the more proper Miss Laerty. Embarrassed. She was embarrassed by the natural mistake. He felt enormously sorry for her situation.

Refolding the letter, he slipped it in the envelope and dropped it in the box beneath his bunk.

"So?"

He looked over at Cam.

"What did she have to say she couldn't have said to me to pass along?"

"An apology. Rather unnecessary, but very hospitable."

"Apology for what, pray tell?"

"For the assumption she made, or understood from Miss Monroe's indiscretion of talking too freely."

"She wrote to apologize for thinking you were the father? She didn't tell anyone?"

"If she did, she didn't say so."

"She wouldn't." Cam got out of his bunk and paced around the small tent. "She wrote to apologize to you but sent nothing to me. Did she mention me?"

"Only to say Miss Monroe will be happier when you return so she can be with her husband and child's father as she should be. Nothing more."

"Her husband." Cam shoved a hand through his hair. "How can I be? My heart is full of Maura. I hardly know Sadie."

Abe raised his eyebrows. "It's my understanding you know her better than you know Miss Laerty, unless you compromised two women before you left."

"How could you think such a thing? I was trying to marry her. Maura is a lady. She would never…"

"And so is Miss Monroe." Abraham stood and walked up face to face with his friend. "You're right about one thing, Cam. You don't know Sadie. Maybe she does not come from a high class family. Maybe she has no money to speak of. But she is a lady. Smart. Sweet. Good-natured. She did not deserve what you have put her through, and although I remain your friend since you are standing up as well as you can by now, I will never fully forgive you for what you have done."

"But it wasn't only me. You know I would never force myself on anyone. The girl was quite willing, flirtatious."

"She was upset."

"As was I."

Abe walked away. He knew his friend was right. He knew Sadie had to have agreed. Still, Cameron wasn't the one stuck in town where everyone now looked down on her, thrown out of her house, having a baby without a legal father. She would pay for it much more than Cameron would. A gentleman would have considered the risks and refused to take them.

"You have more feeling for her than you wish to admit." Cameron closed in from behind.

It felt like a dare. Abe refused to turn. "I have feelings for her.

They used to be moral, respectful feelings. Now they are regretful."

"Abe, if you had told me how you felt about her, I never would have…"

"You shouldn't have anyway."

"You're right. I shouldn't have. And I will pay for it forever. Unless … no one but the four of us know I'm the father. If you have feelings enough for her…" Cam walked around to face him. "You could marry her and claim to be the father. She would be happier. It's you she wants. And…"

"No."

"Abe…"

"She carries your child."

"And you would take it out on the child?"

"I would never. But you would have us lie to your child?"

Cam shrugged. "You'll be the better father. It would be a gift to him."

Abe stared while he considered knocking Cam to the ground. Then he shook his head. "No. You learn to be a good father. And you learn to be a good husband. You owe them that."

+_+_+

Maura peeked out the window around the curtain. They were still there. Holding signs and yelling occasional curses, the crowd appeared determined to stay as long as anyone might still see them. What good did they think it would do to stand outside the home and throw epithets at wounded soldiers and young mothers? They made no laws. They could change nothing. And if they did believe what they had done for their country was right, it was their right to believe so, and do as they did. It was also the right of those who disagreed with the war to do so, and yet, no one held signs in front of their houses and places of business cursing them for believing opposite.

If Maura had more strength and better ability to protect herself, she would consider writing the names of the few faces she recognized and holding a rally in front of each of their homes in protest of their refusal to go and fight themselves, to help protect their right to voice their own opinions. She imagined they would deem it unfair of her.

With a sigh, she released the curtain and stepped back. She needed to return to her own home, to get dinner. Sadie had been too fatigued and held too much ache in her body to stand long enough to take care of any meal more than a slice of toast and a two minute egg.

Maura would simply have to get through them and force herself not to answer their accusations.

Slipping her long apron off, she set it in the wash pile and straightened her hair. She had stopped bothering with the way it mussed during the day and instead left it until she went out into public view. The younger girls who constantly fussed about their appearance when work was to be done gave her no end of annoyance. The mothers and babies paid no heed to their looks, and the soldiers did not have need to do so until they were healed and out on their own.

Maura sighed again. She'd become a true dour spinster already. It was good for the young men to have the distraction of flirting with their caregivers. She knew it was. But each week, she received less of it herself and her father's words of becoming too worn out to gain a man's attention rang through her mind. Now that Cameron was fully off limits, what was she left with? Possibly, she would move. She could sell off the house, clean out the bank account, and start over elsewhere, somewhere bigger with more opportunities. Once Cameron came back to collect Sadie and the child, it would be possible.

She wrapped her heavy shawl over her shoulders as she pondered the idea and headed toward the door. "Good night, Miss Jeanne. I'm off for home."

"Oh, Maura dear." The silver-haired home director caught up to her quickly despite the slight limp she always carried. "You mustn't go out alone."

"It is not dusk yet. I have time…"

"But the crowd."

"The crowd will simply have to part and allow me passage. I am in no mood for their blockade."

"Please dear, wait only a few more minutes. Mr. Hardy will be along to deliver a few supplies and I'll insist he drop you at home, or at least past these ne'r-do-wells. I don't trust them as far as I can spit."

Maura gave the kindly woman a light hug and grin. "I will be well, thank you. Mr. Hardy will be thirty minutes at best and I am simply too interested in finding home and a meal long before then." Rushing off before Miss Jeanne could argue, Maura yanked her shawl tighter and shivered at a slap of bitter wind.

"There's one!"

She looked up toward the voice. It stared back at her and gathered those around it. With a quick scan, Maura headed away from the main path and ducked around the side of the building, her steps fast, hands pulling tightly on the edges of her wrap. Shouts of "war mongerer" and "evil nurser" followed behind. She didn't look back. She did keep her chin up as far as the wind would allow. She would not let them know they bothered her.

As she noticed several strangers heading her way from her side, Maura quickened her pace. It was the cold, she insisted. She wished to be home out of the cold, nothing more.

Their movement directly in front of her made her halt. "Excuse me, you are blocking my path." She forced her chin to stay high.

One of them stepped closer, a scraggly young man who needed a shave and a bath. "We had every intention of blocking your path. We have every intention of prohibiting you from helping those murderers inside, as well. Whatever means it takes." He took another step. The two behind him followed.

"I care for new babies and their mothers. Would you not have them receive care? They have done nothing."

"Babies." The boy who was a head taller than Maura eyed her. "You don't help those murdering soldiers none?"

"I do as I am asked when I am at work, as did they. Now, if you'll excuse me…"

He grabbed her arm.

"Remove your hand!" She felt herself yanked nearly off her feet, her face smashing into his hard shoulder. His arm shoved into her back to hold her against him. She pushed against him as well as she could, her heart pounding, her father's words to be wary smacking into her brain.

A gun shot loosened the grip.

"Let her alone and back off before I put a hole through each of your skulls."

The boy released her. Maura yanked her wrap back around her shoulders and closed it in front, shivering, stumbling backward.

"Go on now. Move along. And do not bother any other of the ladies from the home, as I'll be here watching." A deep, strong voice accompanied the cock of a rifle.

Maura dared a glance toward the man. He was older than she would have expected, and familiar. His hair grayed at the temples but was still largely deep brown. His eyes were kind when they turned to her. She gave him a nod. "Thank you."

He took only two paces closer. "Are you harmed?"

"No. I am … only cold. And I am very grateful." She studied his face. It was quite familiar. Gathering her nerve, she moved close enough to offer a hand. "I am Maura Laerty, and I feel like we've met, but I'm afraid I'm not quite sure. We only moved here a few years past."

"Ah, so you are the betrothed of my son's wilder friend. A Mr. Terry, I believe."

"I am not." It came out harsher than she meant. "My apologies. I suppose I am a bit shaken. I meant to say, I am not betrothed to Mr. Terry. It is only…." Maura frowned. His friend? "You're Abraham's father?" A blush crept into her face. She ducked her head. "My apologies again. You are Mr. Luchner?"

"I am Abraham's father, and I don't believe he would mind use of the name his mother and I gave him."

"Oh, I didn't mean to be improper. I only … Mr. Terry has spoken of him so often and so well, I tend to forget we haven't met." She shivered at a gust of wind.

"Cameron has a kind heart, despite his upbringing. He has always been welcome in our home. Please, allow me to drive you home before you catch a chill."

"Thank you, I'm not far away. I always walk. It is good for the soul and for the heart, so they say."

His mouth curled at the edges. "So it is. And yet I have held you up much longer than I should have and the cold grows worse. This one time, it would do no harm to accept a very small kindness in return for what you do here." He nodded toward the home.

"I am glad to do it. I only wish I could do more."

"Please." He offered his arm, the one not holding his rifle, and walked her a few steps to where a large deep red, slightly rusted automobile stood out against the dulled brown-green of hibernated grass and bare trees and the gray street.

She was highly relieved, as he closed the door behind her, to be out of the wind. He walked around in front and climbed behind the wheel, starting it with a patient hand and a light prod.

"Do you actually plan to stay outside the home and watch until those people go away?"

"I do."

"May I ask why you would? Do you know someone who

works there? Family?"

"My only family is away fighting. I know no one there. I only know how necessary your work is, and the work of everyone in that home. I do it for my son, and for the son of every other parent who hopes for the safety and health of their children. For all of us thankful for what you do. I came into town this morning as soon as I heard. And I am not the only one here watching."

Maura was struck silent. As he pulled in front of her house and walked around to open her door, she wondered how like his father Abraham was. And then she shoved the thought aside. "Would you like to come in for some hot tea to warm you?"

"Thank you, but I must be back at my post in case of further trouble. I doubt there will be any tonight, since word of a rifle travels quickly and ruffles the feathers of bullies rather well."

"Yes, I suppose it would. My thanks again. And my best wishes for your son's safe return."

He gave her a light nod and stood guard until she was inside.

"Is that old Mr. Luchner?" Sadie pulled her head from the window.

"Yes. He caught me headed home and offered a lift. Very kind man."

"He is very kind. Always more polite to anyone than they deserve."

Maura searched her face. "You have met?"

"Of course. He used to be in town often. Everyone knows him. Everyone who has been here long enough, that is."

"Oh. I suppose they would." At times, Maura nearly forgot she was a newcomer. She wouldn't tell Sadie of the trouble at the home, or precisely why Mr. Luchner offered her assistance. The girl didn't need more worries than she had already. "If you don't mind, I'll head up for a quick bath before dinner, as the cold has penetrated all the way through."

"You should stay in when the weather is this bad, Maura. You'll catch your death and they'll tell you they have no time to come and be of assistance to you. Just you watch and see."

"I'm sure that's not true, but I have no plans to find out." With a light grin, she said a hello to Rudy and padded up the cold wooden stairs.

twelve

"Rudy!" Sadie lowered onto the settee, her arms supporting the weight of her protruding stomach. Was it labor already? There should still be two weeks left. She wanted those two weeks. She wasn't hardly prepared for this. Truth be told, she would be no better prepared in two weeks. Maura had at least set up the basics, a small bassinet and supply of diapers.

Sadie had gone to her mother, to try to claim her own baby items she knew her mother saved for Sadie's children. The woman not only refused her entrance, but also the clothing and blankets. She was in tears upon returning to Maura's. Maura begged her not to be concerned, that the child would have what it needed. Maura's kindness oft made Sadie more guilty than if she'd told her to get out after she found who fathered the child.

"What is it Miss Sadie?" Rudy ran into the room and stopped wide-eyed in front of her.

"Run to the home and get Maura. Please. Run fast."

He nodded and ran out the door.

Sadie cradled her stomach during a series of sharp pains. It wasn't labor. It was too sharp. Anyway from what she heard it was too sharp. Maura was concerned about how badly Sadie had been feeling, no matter how she tried to brush it off as only part of the burden. Sadie couldn't help think it might be better if the baby didn't live. With the letter she planned to write to Cameron, she knew it would be unfair to keep the child and she wasn't sure she could let him go. But she wanted him. He wasn't Abraham's as she'd always hoped, but he was hers. She would find a way to care for him.

Clenching her eyes, she wasn't sure if it was more from the physical pain or the mental. Abraham's friend. Why had she done such a stupid thing? She'd asked herself the same every day since it happened, since the one drink she had impaired her judgment and made her turn too far to Abe's friend while longing so hard for Abe. She loved him. He had barely spoken to her but she loved him all the same. The way he walked. His quiet voice. His sturdy shoulders and strong back. The curve of his nape. The lightness of his sun-bleached hair and green of his eyes. A handsome man who didn't act handsome. An intelligent man who didn't talk down to her. When he did speak to her, he looked into her eyes, not down at her full breasts as every other young man did. A gentleman but not a dandy, not....

The pain. The pain grew more intense. She had to stop thinking of him.

And yet, she knew she must write him. She owed him that. She believed he did have even the slightest of feelings for her and must now truly hate her for what she'd done. Would he still speak to her at all? She wouldn't blame him if not. She would never dare approach him. It would be his right to avoid any contact. All the more reason for her to send Cameron the letter she intended.

Maybe she would write Abraham first. She could do so while she waited for Maura. Her friend could possibly not leave immediately. The letter would distract her from ... from the attacks of pain.

The desk was nearby. She could get that far.

Her arms were weak as she tried to put all of her weight on them. Movement added to her discomfort and she gave up on the idea. She'd write Abraham later.

She closed her eyes and pressed her hands against the worst of the pains.

"*Sadie.*" Maura rushed in with Rudy on her heels and knelt in front of her. "Are you in labor?"

"I'm not certain."

"Is the pain dull or sharp?"

"Sharp. Very sharp." She clenched her eyes at the strongest one yet.

"Constant or in intervals?"

"Constant. Sudden. Maura, it's not labor. Something is not right. I am being punished for what I've done."

"Of course you are not. You tried to do more than you should, against my orders. Come. You need to see the midwife. Perhaps she will enforce your rest as I've been unable. Rudy, run next door and ask Mr. Weathers if he would kindly drive us. Sadie, you'll have to make it out to the sidewalk. I'll help you. Give me your arm."

+_+_+

A letter from Sadie? Cameron eyed it the way Abe had eyed the one Maura wrote him. Abe must have seen it, as it was on his bunk and not the stand. Their mail boy set mail on the stand. Only Abe set it on the bed.

His friend was already asleep, or nearly. Cameron tried to get him to join him in the rec tent for a beer or two, but Abe, as always, refused. His rest and quiet were more of value, he said.

With a shrug, Cameron tossed a glance at his friend, kicked out of the boots he'd come to despise, and plopped down on his own bunk to tear the letter open.

Mr. Terry,

I had nearly decided not to contact you after your letter to me, but with things as they are, I feel I must. I am, at this moment, lying in a very unprivate bed in the midst of many women who have recently delivered babies and listening to children play in the next room. I am at the home where Maura works. This is temporary, if all goes well, and I will return to Maura's. I hope I can, more for her than for me. She does not wish to be alone and I do not wish for her to be alone.

I am here because I have not been well. The doctor says it is mental strain due to lack of a husband's support. I know he is only making a point and I promptly demanded he not speak to me that way again. Maura was embarrassed, I believe, but I will not be spoken down to. You and I do not know each other and so you will not understand my pride given my current conditions. However, it is still fully intact, or at least intact enough.

Further, I have tucked the money you sent into a small box for safe-keeping for my child. I will not touch it myself. I nearly returned it to you, as I know you do not want me more than I want you. I do not blame you for what happened. It was my fault as well. However, I know you continue to write to Maura and likely still wish for her to take you back. She will never lower herself to do so. You are wasting your ink. And you have made me realize I can never take you as a husband as long as you want another, even another you cannot have.

Please do not worry yourself over coming home to a marriage you do not want. I will not have you. I will live on my own and make do with my child. I am quite capable and I no longer care what anyone in town will say. I had thoughts of moving elsewhere, making up a story of a lost husband. There are so many, no one would think anything of it. However, Maura is intent on helping with the child and I dare not break her heart by moving away. I also see no reason I should run. Think what they like, I am worth as much as any of them and shall hold my head up and raise my child to be proud of who he is.

I am tired and must rest, but first I do have one thing for which I must ask of you: when you write your family, kindly ask them to keep their tongues in their mouths and to never speak to me again. You are free to ask them why I make this request if you like.

Sadie

Cameron rubbed his eyes, grimaced at the sand that fell in from some crease or from his fingers and blotted it out again, then stared at the letter. She wouldn't have him? What did she mean she wouldn't have him? She darn well would have him. She carried his child. She would not live alone with the infant in squalor somewhere instead of allowing his care.

She was right. Maura would never have him. Neither would anyone else of any … anyone with any decency. None would have him. What did she mean of his family? He'd asked only that they offer support. What was the harm in that? They hadn't bothered to reply, but then, they had yet to write to him at all, despite several letters he sent.

Sadie and his child, their child, were all he had left. And Abe. Except Abe would always be angry with him, at least in part. He would be angrier if Cameron allowed Sadie and the child to be on their own.

Cameron didn't want them on their own.

As tired as he was, and as much as his eyes burned from cold and sand and smoke, he rustled through his box for paper and pen.

Dear Sadie,

Since you have thrown propriety out the window, I feel no need to use it myself.

I am unsure why you were offended by the offer of help from my family. It is my duty to help care for my child and since I am not there, it falls on my family for the time being. I will write to them, as you suggested. However, since they refuse to write in return, I'm afraid I will remain lost as to why you are upset unless you explain yourself. If you do not wish to do so, I will hold no guilt at being unable to make amends.

I am tired, as well, and I am also part laid up. I have managed to injure my back, enough to be in constant pain but not enough to be unfit for the job. I refuse to use what small amount of pain killer we have available, as there are many who need it more. They say this is a permanent injury, so I may as well get used to overlooking it.

However, I am concerned about your health more, and the health of my ... of our child. I am sure Maura will take good care of you and insist the doctors do the same. But please do not strain yourself. If you cannot speak to my family, in which case I am curious as to why but not entirely surprised as I do not often wish to speak to them myself, then at the least ... I suppose your mother still will not give in?

Cameron set the pen down and looked over at his friend. "Hey."

Abe didn't bother to raise his head. "What?"

"I have to ask you a favor. Are you awake?"

"No. Go to sleep, Cam. It's up early tomorrow."

"I got a letter from Sadie."

"As I saw. Is she well?"

"No."

Abe sat up.

"Glad you're awake."

"I'm not. What is it? Why is she not?"

"She's in the home with doctors looking after her. She had complications, but she's doing well, so she says, although I think there is more behind what she doesn't say."

"The baby?"

"She didn't say, but she does talk of caring for him." Cameron tilted his head. "Are you sure you wouldn't like to offer to be the father? I'm quite sure she would rather have you."

"I am quite sure I will not take over your responsibility while you are well able to manage yourself. Then all is well and you startled me awake for no purpose?"

"Perhaps. But there has been some kind of issue with my family. She asked me to write them and request they not speak to her or speak about her. She didn't say more and I'm not sure if she will. But I'm afraid ... if she needs assistance, more than Maura can provide, she may not have it."

"What do you expect me to do, Cameron?"

"Could I suggest, if ever needed, she could ... I should not ask this and I know I should not. I have nowhere else to turn."

"What?"

"Could she go to your father's to stay if needed?"

Abe peered through the half dark in silence. And then he lay back down. "I am not the father, Cam. Don't try to make this my..."

"I am not asking that. I will take responsibility. I've offered my hand. She turned me down, says she won't have me, but we are not finished with that conversation. I will write to the town council and tell them I am the father and have asked for her hand, if you wish, if you're worried of my intentions..."

"I don't wish that. Why my father?"

"There is nowhere else. And only if there comes a reason she cannot stay with Maura. I see no reason it would happen..."

"Cam. Write your family. Tell them you expect them to be civil, to be responsible..."

"Hell Abe, do you know why you have never been to the house? Why I don't allow it? Because responsible is not something Terrys know the meaning of. I am the most responsible of them all and that's a pathetic admission, I realize. Even if they would take her in, I would not wish it on her. I only asked that they send money since it is easier than to send it from here. Nothing more. I think they haven't."

"All right." Abe mumbled from beneath the blanket. "Tell her, if she must, she can go to my father and explain. He would never turn her away. Now let me sleep, if you will."

thirteen

"Would you just read this letter? How impertinent can a man be?"

Maura raised her eyes toward Sadie without halting her scrub of the floor's corners. She should hire someone. Her father would despair, though. Throwing money away, he would say. Maura wasn't certain she wasn't ready to throw everything away. All of it. The house. The volunteer work at the home. Sadie, who grew less tolerable each day as she grew more round and had been restricted from being on her feet more than a few minutes.

"Read this for yourself." She stuck the letter in Maura's face.

"Can't you read it to me? I need to finish before I can no longer make myself."

"Oh Maura, leave it. The corners make no difference. No one comes anyway. Why bother yourself so?"

"Because I cannot look at it. Papa left the house to me to care for. I intend to keep it the way it's always been kept."

"Then let Rudy do it."

"Rudy is out gathering wood. He will be much too tired by the time he comes in from the cold and the effort."

"I'll read it then. Maybe it will at least keep your mind off what you're doing." Sadie shook the papers to straighten them and cleared her throat as though it needed to be cleared.

Dear Miss Monroe, I have just received your letter and while I understand your thoughts on the matter and cannot blame you for not wanting one second more to have to deal with me, I must insist you rethink the matter. Live by yourself, you say? With my child, I would remind you. That does give me a voice in the issue, like it or not. You did the same act as I to create this issue and so have as much responsibility to make a wise choice for our son. Or daughter, if that be the case.

With all due respect, I beg your forgiveness for whatever my family has done to create such anger. Often, I am far more comfortable right here in the midst of surrounding enemies than I ever was at home, and please understand I cannot control their actions. I will continue to send money, as I have this time, and if you put it away for the child, that is your right. At least I will know you have it available.

Miss Monroe – Sadie – you are right that we do not know each other and I cannot ask you to accept me in that light. Therefore, I shall continue to write and allow you to become acquainted with me as much as is possible considering our situation. As long as I fear we will be here in this … in this place, we shall likely know each other much better through letters than many do through normal courting. Answer if you wish. Of course you are under no obligation to write me. I do hope you will, if for no other reason than I will know my child's mother.

Will you do me one small favor? Please relay to Miss Laerty that I shall no longer bother her with correspondence as it is not proper and I should not want to injure her more than I have already. You are free to share with her whatever you wish.

With all humility,
Cameron

"Now I ask again." Sadie shifted her weight in the chair. "Is that not impertinent? To think I could know him well enough through letters to accept him as he wishes. Hm. When pigs fly."

Maura stood to rinse out the cloth. "It was a very gentlemanly letter, I think."

"Gentlemanly?"

"Yes. No presumptions, and with understanding of how you feel. You should at least read his letters when they come. You may find he would not be a burden to you as you expect." Maura turned to hide her moist eyes when Sadie came to her.

"I thought you were over him. I am sorry…"

"I am. There is nothing to be sorry for. As I said, I was unsure of … I only … it would be nice to have a man's interest again. By the time this is all over, as Father always warned, I will be too worn down and unattractive to gain the favor of any man who…" She set the rag down and headed out of the kitchen and hurried up to her room. It was only fatigue. She didn't need a man's attentions. She needed rest. Quiet.

Peace.

A knock forced her eyes open. She was startled by the bare bit of early light that streamed in from the shutters. Morning? Maura sat up and realized she was still in her house clothes from the night before. She'd only meant to close her eyes for a few moments, to compose herself. She didn't intend to sleep so early, and dressed.

"Miss Maura?" Rudy's young voice sifted through the door.

She stood and straightened herself. "Yes. Come in."

The boy nudged the door and peeked his head around. "Miss Sadie sent me up to check on you. She was afraid you might need help?"

"Thank you, Rudy. No. I'm afraid I fell asleep last night instead of returning as I should have. I didn't get dinner. I hope you found something and didn't go hungry."

He scuffed his feet against the wood plank floor. "Miss Sadie made us a meal. Yours is in the icebox. I don't suppose you'd want it this early."

"Sadie cooked? She is supposed to stay off her feet other than moving from one room to the other."

"She said it was all right. She said she needed to help you more before you collapse and we have no way to care for you." Rudy threw a cautious gaze. "Miss Maura, you won't leave us, will you? Miss Sadie and I and the baby would be in a dreadful fix if you did. And … and I would miss you nearly like I miss my own mama."

"Oh." Maura walked over and pulled the boy into a tight grip. "Do not worry yourself, Rudy. I am not leaving you and I will not collapse. Sadie worries herself too much. It's not good for her. You tell her that when she starts in. Neither of you need to worry. I will be here. And I'll take care of everything. All is well."

Maura stroked his hair and sent him to tell Sadie she would follow in a moment, then she lowered onto her settee. It was only a bad night. She deserved one now and then. Today would be better. She would make it better.

"Come." Maura, washed and dressed, whisked into the sitting room. "We're going on an outing today. It's fine time we had some fun. Rudy, dear, run ask Mr. Weathers if he and Susanna and Tony would like to accompany us to the canyon. If he'll drive, we'll pack a picnic lunch and go enjoy the brisk-warm March air that tells us spring is on its way. What do you both say? Sadie, are you up to an outing?"

"Oh Maura, I can't tell you how wonderful it sounds. But you're not working today?"

"No. I am not working. They can do without me for one day. I have earned the day off."

"Haven't I been telling you so?" Sadie grinned and supported her roundness with one arm as she waddled toward the kitchen. "I'll help you pack the lunch."

"You'll do no such thing. Sit as the doctor ordered and save your strength for getting to the car and out of it again."

"Nonsense. I feel wonderful. And it's been ages since I've packed a picnic. I want to enjoy every moment."

Maura didn't argue. Sadie did appear healthier. Perhaps she had rested enough to allow whatever troubled her to heal well. And the fresh air would be good for the baby, too. Fresh air was what they all needed, more than anything. Freshness. Nature. The sound of water trickling from within the mountains and down the canyon.

The drive was slow and easy. Maura knew Mr. Weathers was nervous with Sadie in his car because of all the bumps and holes along the road, but he was going too slow to bother Sadie or to hit anything that would possibly bother her. It took far too long to go the short distance, but they were soon parked close to a nice picnic spot where they could see across to the jagged rocks on the canyon's far edge.

As soon as the blankets and Sadie were all settled, Maura walked up along the grassy incline close enough to look down into the magnificent river. It was thicker and wider than normal with snow melt adding to its flow. She noted tiny streams that worked their way through crevices in the huge rock walls. This was her favorite place. If she ever had enough leisure time again, she would come sit out here and spend the afternoon by herself admiring the serenity of the strength. Of birds swooping through the air. Of rock chucks scampering from one place to another. Of the magnitude. It always made her troubles feel insignificant. There were always larger things someone had to deal with. Even Sadie had larger problems.

Although perhaps she didn't. Cameron could be quite convincing when he tried. He'd nearly even convinced Maura she loved him when she didn't. Sadie was less ... less apt to be able to resist his charms, especially as she carried his child. Silly thought, Maura admonished herself. Sadie already succumbed to his charms once. It would be easy enough to do so again.

Maura blushed at the thought. She'd meant only ... no, she'd meant exactly what made her blush. And there was no need to blush. It was hardly a secret. Sadie was at nine months. Nothing was still hidden.

With a sigh, she returned to where Susanna had the picnic feast set out. Sadie seemed not horribly comfortable on the small folding chair Maura had brought along for her, but the girl couldn't sit on the ground. Maybe she could get down there with help, but getting up again could cause problems. Maura didn't need one more problem.

Even though she had readied it, with some small help from Sadie, Maura couldn't help being delighted by the taste of everything, the sweetness and saltiness, the sour of the pickles, the tang of the mustard. She enjoyed the laughter of the two boys as they teased and poked fingers into the other's side. Tony was three years older than Rudy but they got along well and Mr. Weathers and his daughter were among the few who allowed Rudy over to their house. Because of Sadie. Yes, she would have a hard road before her if she didn't accept Cameron. Maura hoped she would.

But she would think of it no longer during their picnic. It was a relaxation day. A fun day. She would also not let her conscience tell her it was wrong to have such a nice time while all those boys were still out there. It wouldn't hurt them any. And it wouldn't help anyone the tiniest bit to be morose every day. There was enough morose in the world. More fun was what they needed.

They stayed late, until dusk began its approach and cold warned its coming. Too late, perhaps. Sadie did appear tired as she shuffled up the porch steps with Rudy supporting her arm.

As she settled in and let Sadie know she would throw together a quick dinner, Maura couldn't help think of Rudy and how he had changed toward Sadie. He was polite still, but more distant. More wary. It was her sharpness, Maura supposed. She didn't mean it, but at times Sadie's despair and discomfort caused her tone to be too sharp. Maura hoped it hadn't hurt his feelings. She would have to talk with him about it.

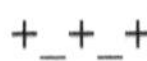

Abraham ducked down into the foxhole and checked the men around him. They all looked uninjured. Close call. Too close. He'd thought for sure this one would be his time. Not that he hadn't thought so before.

Shaking sand off his uniform and shoving it off the top of his helmet, he waited for another blast. They were to stay still until ordered otherwise. He guessed it would be a long wait, and dark would soon fall. The last thing he wanted was another dark night in a foxhole, awake and tuned to every small sound. He wanted to be home, to walk up to the canyon and peer over its edge, to see its trickle of water so far below. Perhaps there would be someone in the midst of it fishing, and children running along the grass atop laughing and playing as they should. He could see it. He could put himself there if he allowed. He couldn't. It was his job to listen. To notice. Anything.

Another promotion had made him a corporal. He wasn't sure he wanted it. He wanted to be home. Someone else could have the honor they said it was.

Of course it was. He knew it was. And if he didn't go home, he'd made sure they all knew to send his rank with his belongings to his father so he would know. His father would be proud. Cameron was still a PFC. So were many others. A few had risen to Specialist. Cam was too mouthy. Too unpredictable.

Nothing like what someone of Maura's temperament needed.

Abe shook off the thought. Maura now wrote to him. Why, he wasn't sure, but the first she sent told him of a grand day at the canyon with Sadie and neighbors and the boy Sadie had taken as her own. As though she didn't have her hands full enough with Cameron's child.

Her descriptions were nearly as beautiful as the way he saw it. Maybe as beautiful. She loved it as he did. Abe couldn't help but read the letters each night. He supposed he shouldn't. But Cam no longer seemed to mind as Sadie now wrote back to him, under Maura's suggestion, she said.

"Hey." Cam shoved a boot into his leg.

"Shh. They're close."

"Yeah, but I have to tell you something."

"What? Are you injured?"

"Me? Injured?" Cam laughed quietly despite Abe's second warning to hush. "You know I haven't read you Sadie's letters."

"Cam. Stop talking."

"I can't."

"Yes you can. Close your lips."

"I don't like dark and I don't like tight spaces. Never told you that, did I? I have to talk so I don't flip out."

"Talk to yourself. Not out loud." He heard something nearby and shoved Cam to prevent whatever he was going to say. And he waited. Listened. With a motion to let the others know to be ready, weapons in position, it felt like forever in the hole in the growing dark. Maybe they waited for dark. He wondered how many there were.

_+_

Abe walked around the medical tent to check the injured. Cam had a gash in his left arm but joked that he barely needed that one anyway. The medic said it should heal well and quickly. Only one of his men was in serious condition, watched constantly. Other injuries were of different extents. One would be discharged, as he would no longer be of use in the field. He hadn't been there long. A rash kid. Too young. Too inexperienced. He reminded Abe of Cameron when they'd first met. Cam had grown up fast. He was paying attention better, becoming a decent soldier. His family should be proud. Abe wondered if they would be.

Cam had finished his thought in the midst of fighting, between Abe yelling at him to pay attention and which way to turn. Sadie's letters were full of fire, he'd said, spirited. They made him laugh even as she disparaged Cameron for being pertinent and assuming she might ever have him. Abe had the feeling she did protest a little too often, and yet she continued to write.

fourteen

Maura worked more easily having taken off the day before. She buzzed around the men as they flirted, sometimes rewarding them with a small grin. And why not? She was unencumbered. She no longer could, nor would, mention Cameron, since he no longer had any hold on her. Now that the shock had lifted, she felt lighter knowing he didn't. Even if her father said working so hard would make her too haggard to draw a decent man's attention, the looks she received from her patients – not hers exactly, but those she helped care for – countered that notion. She drew attention again since they had been picnicking once a week, and especially today as she felt so refreshed.

Perhaps they would invite a couple of recovering soldiers with them on their next outing, as the weather had grown warm and inviting by mid April. A few were well enough to walk along the canyon without need of more than watchful eyes. They would leave the home soon, back to their own homes. It was good to finally see so many men return to their lives. Maura ran into some of them in town at times and returned a pleasant greeting. Many of those who had before looked down on her for her work now showed her respect.

Her father would be glad to see it. He wouldn't have had to worry.

Handing a glass of lemonade to one of her favorite patients, a young man with a huge smile and leg too injured to use again, Maura asked how he was.

"Very well, Miss Maura. Thank you. And you look happy today, if I may say so."

"Of course, Trent. Sadie and I had a lovely day out yesterday. It so refreshed my spirits. Maybe one day soon you could join us, with the doctor's permission."

"Miss Maura, would you be flirting with me?"

She laughed. "I'm afraid you're too young. I tend toward the older men, not too much older, mind you, but older. Please don't be offended."

"Oh I was only joshing with you. But what about Miss Sadie? If I can tell you, I do have an eye for her. She's such a vivacious creature, even with her ... present condition. She is unattached, I hear."

"Her present condition is more than a month overdue and she is not so vivacious at the moment. I'm also not sure she is unattached. You see, the father of her child is developing quite an eye for her, as well. I am sorry to have to tell you. But you are young, Trent. You should look for a young woman who is unencumbered and start your own family."

"I don't mind that she's with child. I would be a good daddy, I would. I have helped with my nieces and nephews aplenty. There are a bunch of them. I'm the youngest, you see." He grew more serious. "But I suppose I should wait and see what happens with my brothers. I might have more children to help with than I know what to do about."

"Yes. I know what you mean." Maura gave him a light grin and moved on. She'd avoided the other side of the home much of the time, where the babies were. There were two orphaned infants she wanted to take home. Of course, she couldn't. She had Sadie and Rudy and the little one on the way and no one to help as it was. So she avoided being close to them. It would be too hard to watch them leave with other families if she did. At nearly twenty-four, it was time for her, also, to begin a family. She felt the pull.

There was no young man in town, however, in whom Maura had any interest. Perhaps she would travel. She could take a local girl with her, after Sadie's child was old enough she didn't need Maura's help. She'd hire someone to help with the house while she was away, and simply leave. Where, she didn't know. But suddenly, she had a huge urge to pick up and go. Somewhere. Anywhere. Where there were people she didn't know, healthy young men who didn't need special care, who would care for themselves well and could very well care for her. And would want to. Not in a dependent sort of way. Maura couldn't imagine feeling dependent on any man, not after what she'd been through. Not after she'd become the house owner, the main caregiver, the cook, gardener, maid, decision maker all in one. No. She would need a man who would know how she wanted care, under her own rules, not his.

She nearly laughed. They didn't exist, she didn't believe. They were a fairy tale. And she was no princess. No. She would have to make do and see where life took her. Perhaps as she grew into old maid status, she would become fully scandalous and take a lover now and then. If all else failed.

+_+_+

"Miss Maura! Come fast!"

"What is it, Rudy?" Maura rushed down the hard stairs as much as she could with aching feet. At times, she detested those steps.

"Miss Maura!"

"I'm here Rudy. What is it?"

"It's Miss Sadie. She says the baby is coming!"

The baby. Maura shoved away thoughts of her aching feet and rushed to follow the boy. She hoped it was true this time. Twice before it had been a false alarm and Sadie became even grumpier after having to return home still round and aching.

One look at her friend made Maura think it was no false alarm this time. Sadie was on the settee, leaned back against pillows, pain covering her face. "Maura." Her voice was full of fear.

"It's all right. Relax now. Take my arm. Rudy, go and fetch Mr. Weathers with the car."

"Yes'm."

Maura asked Sadie about the pain, the timing. "We need to get to the home now. As long as you've waited, it may come more quickly than a first baby should." She attempted to guide Sadie up off the couch.

"I can't. It's too much pain."

"I know, but only to the car…"

Sadie shook her head and dropped it behind her.

"Mr. Weathers is out. No one answers." Rudy stared, afraid.

"Then run get a midwife and bring her here. Rudy, tell her to hurry, please." With a shove to the boy's back to get him moving, she sat next to her friend.

"They don't stop." Sadie panted through shallow breaths. "They keep going. And keep going. It's not right. I know from your face it's not right."

"Hush now. Don't get excited. You're under good care. I'll take care of you until the midwife comes."

"She won't come. They didn't come for your father. They won't come for me."

"Of course they will. My father was old. He wouldn't have been saved anyway. You are young and your baby is new. It's not the same. Just breathe. Easy. I'll take care of you."

Sadie screamed at a pain and Maura brushed fingers against the damp forehead. "Let me go get a cold cloth. I'll be back in only a second."

"Maura promise me." Sadie gasped between pains. "If I don't make it..."

"Don't talk that way."

"But if I don't … take care of my baby for me. And I know I shouldn't ask you, but I have no one else."

"You have Cameron. But don't think that way."

"Cameron. Do you think he would bother with the child if I'm not here to make everything proper? I don't want my baby to be sent away to someone I don't know, even if I shouldn't have had him. Promise me, Maura."

"I promise. Everything will be fine and I'll be here. Your baby will be with you and Cameron. Or he'll be with me. I promise, Sadie. I won't let him go to a stranger. There's been enough of that, as I see it." Maura wiped her friend's brow again. "We need to get you to a bed. The settee isn't big enough. You can't be comfortable here."

"No, I can't move. There's too much pain."

"I'll help you. Lean on me." Maura half carried Sadie into the main floor room that had become her father's. Fitting, she expected. A life ended there and a new one would begin there. It would cleanse the bed and the room of death and give it new breath.

Sadie was settled against the pillows by the time Rudy ran in, face red and out of breath.

"Where is the midwife?" Maura looked around behind him frantically.

"None will come. We need to take her to the home. None can be spared to leave."

"We cannot take her in. I barely got her to the bedroom."

"I am sorry, Miss Maura. None will come. I pleaded…"

Sadie yelled with another pain. "I am a fallen woman. I said they would not come."

"You are betrothed to the child's father, and that matters not at all at a time like this. Let me go and I will make someone come."

"*No.* Maura, you cannot leave me. Rudy…" She called the boy to her side. "You help Miss Maura. Whatever she asks of you, you do it without question. You hear me? She needs your help."

"Yes, Miss Sadie."

"And … if anything happens, you will stay with the baby. He'll be your brother, you hear? Where he goes, so will you. You'll help care for him. You will not be alone again."

Maura pushed between. "Don't scare the boy so. Rudy,

everything will be fine. Run along and put some water on the stove for me. A big pot. Turn it up high. And then bring a cold cloth."

As she watched him nod in fear, Maura gave him a light hug. She would have to deliver. She knew. And she could not act as frightened as she was. For Sadie, or for Rudy.

fifteen

Abraham glanced over at his friend as Cam stared at an envelope. "What is it?"

"A letter."

"I see it's a letter. I am not blind."

"From Maura."

Abe sat up. "Maura? I thought she no longer wrote you."

"She does not."

A pang of jealousy rippled through Abe and he fought it back. "Are you going to read it?"

"I cannot. I am afraid of what it might hold." Cameron stood and paced around the small tent. Then he stopped in front of Abe. "You read it."

"It is not marked to me."

"But I cannot. She said she would not write me again, it was too much a betrayal to Sadie. It means it is bad news. Or it means Sadie is done with me and ... and maybe Maura will give me another chance since I tried to do right. Do you think?"

Abe studied his friend. He had plenty of doubt Maura would change her mind. She didn't, from the letters Cam had read to him or from the letters she wrote to Abe, seem the type to easily change her mind.

"Abe?"

"I would not get my hopes up."

"No. But it is hard not to. Although, now it would be a hard choice unless Sadie will absolutely have nothing to do with me as she still sometimes says. Other times ... I think she is swaying. She has incredible spirit, Sadie does. She's impertinent, head strong, fiery ... and I enjoy that in her. Her letters amuse me, annoy me, keep me guessing. I think we will do well if she has not decided she can no longer wait for me. Maybe she has another suitor."

Cameron paced more, then stood at the stove holding the letter over it. "Maybe that's what it is. Sadie has found another who is there for her as I should be and does not wish me to contact her. I will, by George. She has my child. I have the right to see her. To fight for her." He turned to Abe. "Do you not think I am right in this?"

"And Maura?"

Cam frowned, then sighed. "You were right, my friend. I do

not deserve her. And I think I would not make her happy. She needs better."

He walked over and handed the letter to Abe. "Please. Read it. I cannot. It would be a betrayal to Sadie, would it not?"

Trying not to tear it from his friend's grip, Abe gave him a light nod and accepted. He saw Cam's impatience as he carefully tore open only the top edge so as not to spoil the writing on the outside. But he nearly took pleasure in making him wait.

Finally, he unfolded the sheets of paper. They smelled of her.

Dear Mr. Terry,

Please excuse my writing to you, as I said I would not. However, I have no choice but to do so. My words come with difficulty and so I must make them quick before I cannot make myself keep writing. I have already waited two days since ... I have been far too unwilling to write. Please do not be angry with me for this.

Abe stopped and looked up at Cam, hovering near the stove, his eyes wide.

"Go on."

"You should perhaps sit down."

With a nod, Cam obeyed. He sat on his bunk, his gaze hazy but steady. "Go on. She has left me, hasn't she?"

Abe grabbed a deep breath and returned to the letter.

Sadie's child – your child – was delivered five weeks late, and with complications. No midwife would come to the house and it came upon Sadie much too quickly for me to get her to the home. I had trouble enough, with no help, getting her to the bed, to what was my father's room. I had such hoped the new life would cleanse the room. Maybe it has. For now, I have trouble seeing so.

As I said, no one more prepared and trained for a delivery could come, or would come. I have not been able to force myself to bring a complaint or even speak with them. After all the hours I put in, I did believe...

That's neither here nor there. Excuse my rambles. I am avoiding what I do not wish to tell you.

Let me start with the good news, then. You have a daughter: a beautiful, healthy daughter. I can see your eyes as I look at her.

Abe looked over at Cameron. "Congratulations are in order."

"Go on."

I believe you and Sadie were corresponding happily. At this moment, I wish you had not been, as this would be less difficult for you to hear and for me to tell you. Sadie was not well toward the end. She had much pain. I could not stop the bleeding. I tried everything I have seen during difficult deliveries but I'm afraid I did not do something as I should have.

The funeral was held this morning. She was buried well. I made sure of it.

I am so very sorry, dear Cameron. Please be assured I will care for the child until you come home to take her under your own care. Sadie insisted I not allow her to go to a stranger and I could not bear to allow it. I will treat her as my own until you are home, then.

I must close here with more apologies. For your loss. For my ineptitude that caused your loss. I shan't forgive whatever error I made and I shall miss Sadie as though she was my sister, as I came to feel she was.

Directly, as I am able, I will address the home and find out why a midwife was not sent. It matters not, I suppose. Still ... still.

Be aware the child and I are not here alone. Master Rudy has become more helpful each day. Sadie had beseeched him to stay with her child who is to be like his sister. He is taking on the role well, doing everything he can to help. She adores him already and lies in his arm admiring his face. We will be well until your return.

As you mourn, please remember this beautiful life you helped to create who waits here at home for you. She will bring you many years of joy and memories.

Be well, Cameron, and do not think of me too harshly.
Maura

Silence penetrated the tent even with the wind gushing up against the canvas and quivering the flaps. Abe folded the letter and placed it back inside the envelope. He dared not return it to Cameron as of yet. It would very well end up on the fire. Abe could not allow it. Instead, he set it on his own stand and went to sit next to his friend. "You have a daughter."

Cam nodded, his expression unreadable.

"Maura will take good care of her."

"Yes."

"Cam. I am sorry. I believe you had started to fall for her..."

Cam shot up off the bunk and shoved both hands through his hair. "I've killed her. This was my doing. I was irresponsible and ... and now she's dead and I've killed her. She was so lively, so full of life, of energy. How could this happen? Fall for her? Yes, more than started. I did fall for her. I looked forward to going home just to be with her, with our child, to build the kind of family I wished I'd had, the kind that ... that would forgive, that would care, that would understand. We could have had that, Sadie and I and the baby."

"You still can."

"How?"

"You have a daughter. You will, eventually, fall for another girl who will be glad to be a mother for your child, who will want the same kind of family you want..."

"No." Cam darted out the tent.

Abe followed and grabbed him. "Cam, you can't go walk around out here in the dark. With no helmet and no weapon? It would be suicide."

"I killed her, Abe. As well as if I did the deed purposely."

"No. You did nothing but give her a child. Her medical matters were not your doing. The home's refusal to send a midwife was not your doing..."

"They wouldn't because she was not married. You know they care less..."

"Not at the home. Cam, that's much of what is there. Mothers alone. Unmarried, with nowhere to go. It cannot be the reason. There must have been an emergency, too much happening..."

"Don't excuse them. Even Maura doesn't excuse them. You read her letter. She is angry with them, as she should be, as I should be..."

"Fine." Abe grabbed his shoulders and stood in his face. "You be angry at them, as is your right. Go home as soon as we can go home and find out why. Be angry. But do not let it eat at you. Only let it spur you to do what you must. We'll finish this soon. The better we can do our jobs, the sooner we'll finish this and go home. To your daughter. Think of that, Cam. Think of her."

Cameron's face relaxed; his body started to slump. "Think of her. Maura didn't even tell me her name. I do not know what my child is called."

"Write to her and ask."

Abe waited two days to allow Cameron time enough to grieve before he pushed him to write to Maura. She needed a response. Still, he refused. He wouldn't even do so to find out the name. He thought it might be easier not to know.

"If you do not write her tonight, I will write her."

Cam raised his eyebrows. "You haven't written her once in all the times she's written you, content to have me pass a simple thank you for the letters through Sadie. Why would you write her now? You do not even write your father."

"My father is not raising someone's child and feeling guilty about not saving the mother. She has no reason to feel guilty. You should tell her so."

"You tell her so."

Abe stared a moment. "Fine. I will tell her so." Pivoting, he went to Cameron's box and pulled out paper.

"You find it all right to dig through my things now?"

"I have no writing paper, as I had no intentions of writing. You should do this." Abe thrust it toward him. Cam reclined on his bunk and closed his eyes.

With a frown, Abe returned to his own, propped a book beneath the paper, and considered how to start.

Dearest Miss Laerty,

Accept my apology for writing to you in place of Mr. Terry. He received your letter and thanks you deeply for sending it, but he is still too overwhelmed by the events to be able to write. I do hope you understand, as he had developed quite a fondness for Miss Monroe and had looked forward to building a family with her.

I am sure he will respond on his own in time. However, I believe it unfair to make you wait for a response that long, since it already takes too long for mail to reach you from here. By the time you read this, I would imagine you have settled in with your new role of adoptive mother and the two of you are managing well. Three. Beg my pardon. It is a comfort you have young Rudy as assistant. I do have to wonder that you do not hire extra help.

Excuse my intrusion upon your personal affairs. It is not my place to suggest such a thing. However, I do think, if you have the resources, no one including your father would begrudge you further assistance or look down on that in any manner. You have done so much for others, they should return the favor to you without asking. I do not imagine they have. It is regretful.

If you have not crumpled this to throw on the fire, then please allow me to urge you also not to berate yourself for Miss Monroe's loss. Cameron also does not place any blame on you and does not wish you to take blame on yourself. He is thankful you were with her to keep her in company and, I'm sure, as comfortable as possible considering the circumstances. He is also quite grateful for your willingness to look after his child until he is home. He looks forward to meeting his daughter and I am quite sure he will be a good father for her. He wonders why you did not send the child's name. I told him you were sure to be overwhelmed, also, which is to be expected.

Accept my gratitude, if you will, for all that you are doing for Cameron. He will recover knowing you care for things in his place. If not for that, I am quite sure he would be beside himself, and it is so important here that he keep his head clear and alert. That was his biggest struggle when he arrived, but you would be proud to see how far he has come. He should well receive a promotion soon. I look forward to seeing it pinned on him.

I do hope you will take my unwanted advice to gather help for yourself. Cameron will gladly send you support, if you need, which is his duty. Also, although I have not written my father of the situation, I have to assume he knows of Cameron's child and in all likelihood of Miss Monroe's sad fate. If you need, at any time, you could ask for his assistance. Tell him I sent you. I am sure he would be glad of nothing but a small bit of company in return. He would not ask this of you. He would ask nothing. My wish that he provide assistance is all that is required. Please do not hesitate.

It is late now and it has been a grueling day, although not much more so than any other, and so I am off to sleep. Cameron, I believe, is already passed out from exhaustion and worry. Do not be concerned. We are looking after each other and although I should not say it – blame it on the fatigue and homesickness if you wish – but each day is tolerable here only because of your reminders of home and for such care you provide. Cameron's child is lucky, indeed, to be wrapped in such warmth.

With all the best wishes,
Abraham Luchner

Abe sealed the letter quickly before he could change his mind about sending it and then went to Cameron's box to fetch another blank sheet. He had to write his father, to tell him of the offer. And to tell him he was all right and hoped to be home with him soon. He would not promise. He would not be too certain with his phrasing, but he wanted at least to touch his father for just a moment before dawn rose and he was again lost to his work.

+_+_+

Maura stared at the letter for some time, and broke down in tears. She could not make them stop no matter what she tried, what she told herself. *Wrapped in such warmth.* If only she could tell him how much she needed, herself, to be wrapped in such warmth, as his letter had done.

The baby cried in echo, except hers was hunger: plain, pure, simple hunger easily solved. Maura wiped her face as well as she could, then picked her up out of the bassinet and cuddled her against her chest. Her name. Abraham wanted to know her name. She could not tell him since Sadie hadn't given her one. Maura called her Baby. She couldn't bring herself to call her an actual name and then have it changed. Cameron would decide.

Maura had forgotten to ask him.

With a grimace, she laid the baby on the dresser to change her into dry diapers, managing to do it this time without sticking the pin into a finger, and took the child downstairs to get a bottle. A name. It would be two weeks or more before she wrote to Cameron and then waited for a reply. And yet, she didn't wish to write to Cameron. He hadn't even the courtesy to respond to her letter. He'd had Abraham do it.

Well, then, she would write to Abraham and have him relay the message. If he had no response, Maura would name the child.

Cuddling young Miss Terry in her arm – surely Cameron would at least give her his last name – Maura nearly dreaded going in to the home later. She'd gone later and later as time went on, and returned earlier. No one thought anything of it. After all, she had a child to care for and a boy to feed. Rudy had found a way to keep busy while she worked. He was hired by an older gentleman to run errands. Maura didn't know the man's name, but Rudy said he was friendly and paid decent. Word caught on how hard the boy worked and two older widows had also taken to paying for errands: taking care of the yards, running to the store, anything the nine-year-old could do that older legs had trouble with.

It seemed to make Rudy happy. He smiled wide when he

showed Maura his pay and placed most of it in her palm – to help with expenses for the baby, he said. She tried to refuse, but he insisted the baby was his sister as Miss Sadie had told him and it was his job to help care for her in any way he could.

A delightful boy. Maura would well miss him when Cameron showed to take them both home, at Sadie's request. She couldn't imagine he would turn Rudy down. The boy was such help, and good company. And Maura would miss him.

A knock on her door startled her. She never had visitors.

Setting the bottle on the table, she calmed the baby's fuss with a gentle pat on her back and looked out the side window before she opened the door only enough to converse. "Good morning, Madam Ramsey, what can I do for you?"

The plump woman looked over her spectacles at the baby. "That is the child of Sadie Monroe, is it not?"

"Yes."

"Well then, I will have to take her with me to process for adoption."

"No." It came out harsher than Maura meant, as it surprised her so. "I'm sorry. I mean I am to keep the baby here until Mr. Terry returns for her."

"Mr. Terry?"

"Yes. Cameron Terry, her father."

"Sadie was not married to Mr. Terry or anyone else. How do you know he was the father?"

"She said he was."

"And you believe someone of her nature?"

Maura felt her face redden. "Her nature. Madam Ramsay, Sadie's nature was loving, kind, and trusting. She trusted Mr. Terry to do the right thing by her, and as soon as he returns, he very well intends to do so. The child is now his alone and he has asked, as Sadie did, that I care for her until then."

"And you have a letter stating so?"

"A letter."

"Yes, Miss Laerty. A letter. It is not common to allow a single young woman lone care of another woman's child, at least not without going through proper means to make sure the arrangement is acceptable. Since you have worked at the home for so long, you know the requirements."

"But this child was not born at the home. Neither did a midwife from the home bother to come help when we called for it.

Therefore, the home has no say over what happens with this child. She stays with me until her father comes for her and I will not discuss it further."

"Miss Laerty…"

"I have nothing more to say. And if you will, let them know I will not be in today." Maura set a hand on the door. "Good day." She kept her nerves intact until it was shut and bolted and then half fell against it.

"Miss Maura?"

She turned toward the young voice. "Yes Rudy?"

"They can't take my sister away, can they?"

"No, honey. I won't let them. She will go to her father and stay here until then, as I told her. Don't you worry about it. I'll take care of everything."

A letter. They'd asked for a letter as proof. Maura would have to get one in case of trouble.

She would send it to Abraham. He could pass along the request to Cameron, and Cameron could backdate it. Maura didn't want anyone to see a letter going to Mr. Terry the day of Madam Ramsey's visit.

While writing, she sent a separate note to Abraham, one he needn't share. It was improper, she supposed, but his kindness did need to be answered. After sealing it, she wrapped the baby, called for Rudy, and took a walk into town. Her first stop was the post office. Next, she went to inquire about young girls who might need a day or two of work each week. She had told Abraham she would gladly accept his advice since it was meant so sincerely.

+_+_+   Summer II   +_+_+

his Boots
by Catherine Moore

they rest, briefly
in midnight black
camouflaged with dust
from the desert sands
weathered stalwarts
in tents, untied, ready
for duty, though tired,
tattered by arid winds which
crack the soles and run trenches
across toes like the wrinkles
on old men's furrowed brows.

sixteen

Abraham ached from his cropped hair to his little toe. Summer was upon them again, which meant nearly a year had passed since he and Cameron had been in this hell-hole of a place, sleeping with sand and snakes and dung beetles. Everything inside him wanted to scream out as loud as he could manage, but it would only make his parched throat more sore, his cracked lips more cracked. His recent promotion did little to raise his spirits, even if it was so unusual to rise in rank so fast and if his captain pulled a lot of strings to get it through in order to put Abe more in charge. To tell the truth, it did nothing for his spirits. He wanted to go home. He wanted to work the farm, to look out over the land that belonged to him, to his father and to him. To his future family if he were to ever have one. If he were to ever leave this place.

"*Sergeant.*"

Abe turned to see if he was the sergeant being called. A private headed his way, mail in hand.

"For you, Sarge." The boy, barely old enough to be allowed in the Army, handed him two letters.

"Thank you, Private Maine. Rest well tonight. I hear we may move camp early."

"Yes, Sarge. I heard. Do you think it's a good sign?"

Abe set a hand on his shoulder. "I hope so. I'm ready to go home. How about you?"

"I only got here two months ago, Sarge. I have yet to prove what I can do."

"Prove what you can do when you get home. Here, prove you can stay alive."

"Yes, Sergeant." With a nod, he headed off to find others lucky enough to have received mail.

Abraham hadn't dared to look at his own with the boy standing there. Now, he held them in his hands and forgot how to move his feet enough to continue to his tent. His father wrote. As did Maura. With a light clench of his eyes, he willed himself back to where he was and kept from raising her letter to his nose. He wondered if he should tell Cam. His friend was hardly even half himself since the loss of Sadie. Abe was afraid to trigger anything worse in him.

Cam was already in the tent, fully in uniform, boots included, lying on his cot. Staring at the ceiling.

"Hey, at least shower before you sleep. You'll wake up unable to stand your own smell otherwise." Abe tried to tease.

Cam only stared.

Setting the letters, his father's on top, on his stand – the stand he'd made from scrap pieces of wood he'd found lying about – he went to his friend and sat at the edge of the bunk. "You have to pull out of this."

"What's the need? I am doing no one any good, either way. I killed Sadie. I cannot be there to take care of my child. I have lost Maura's friendship so that she no longer will even write me other than with that horrid news. I can't help think part of her took pleasure in being able to tell me what my actions brought about…"

"You cannot believe that." Abe felt his mouth try to gape, but he wouldn't allow it. "She is not a vengeful soul, Cam. You know better. How would you think such a thing?"

He turned his eyes to Abe's, staring, the light hazel seeping deeply into Abe's soul. "You came in with mail. Did she write you again?"

He couldn't lie. He could have hid it if possible, but he wouldn't outright lie to his friend. "Yes." With Cam's nod and continued stare, he tried to move from the subject. "I have a letter from my father, as well."

"Your father?" A touch of Cameron's old self hinted through. "What did he say? Is he well?"

"I've yet to read it. I barely walked into the tent."

"Well, go read it. Why are you bothering with me? I am always here." He gave a sarcastic sniff. "Always here."

"If my father is not well, what do you expect me to do from here? I can do nothing. But you, my friend, are at my side and we are in this together. I will do whatever it takes to pull you out of this. I plan to go fishing only days after we get back and need my partner out there to best me. I still cannot see how we can fish in the same spot with the same tackle and you, every time, catch either the bigger fish or more of them. One day, that will change."

Cam at least gave him a half grin. "Catching has never been my problem, Abe. You know that as well as anyone. It's keeping them after I have troubles with." Another grin, referring – Abe knew – to how often Cameron let the fish slip right out of his fingers once he got them off the hook. He joked it was clumsiness. Abe figured he didn't want to let them die and so pretended they slipped.

"Or at least keeping them alive after." With a silent cringe that revealed how his back still bothered him, although he said nothing, Cameron turned to his other side. "Maura should not write me again. I am not safe."

"Not safe." Abe shoved fingers against his shoulder. "Because of Sadie you are not safe? It was not because of you. Any other man would have been the same result. It was her, or it was circumstances. It was not you. Besides, no one has been around you more than I have and I'm still quite safe." With a tap to his arm, Abe got up. "Stop feeling sorry for yourself and go shower. When you come back, I'll tell you what my father said, but not before you shower."

With a deep sigh, Cameron obeyed.

Abe was glad to get the opportunity to read the letters alone. Unlacing his boots, he tried to decide which to read first. As he pushed them off to thud onto the makeshift floor consisting of excess pieces of the wood he'd gathered laid side-by-side by his cot, he opened his father's letter. He held it, folded, between his fingers for some several seconds before he leaned back against the pillow and focused on the overly-slanted writing. He was out of practice reading the handwriting and had to study it for a moment, but it made him grin; the familiarity was a comfort.

My Dear Son,

I cannot fail to tell you first how glad I was to see your hand on the outside of the letter you sent. I accepted your decision not to write or promise to send word, and while I respect your reasons, I am quite glad to be able to look over and see you on the page whenever I decide. You sound to be well. I pray nightly for your safe return.

As I know the personal words are not comfortable for you, I will leave it there and move along.

I am grateful you wrote about young Cameron and Miss Monroe. There have been questions, as, at first, many said the child was yours. If it were true, I would of course be glad to help care for the child as yours and would have insisted on providing support for the girl. I am, I have to admit, glad to hear the child is not yours as I do believe you have much more responsibility than to leave a girl in such a state. There is a part of me that wished it were yours, however. A grandchild would be a blessing regardless of circumstances. I look forward to the day I can hold your child in my arms.

There I go, getting sentimental again. You will have to forgive a man who has missed his only son for nearly a whole year.

News around town: there is not much to tell. I am afraid you will have your hands full with this old place upon your return. I keep up as I can, but there is only so much I can manage now with my old limbs losing the strength they once had. Do not let this make you feel sorry. I am grateful for every day and also pray you will someday know the joy of having lived long enough to feel your body move closer to the earth and Heaven again. It is an incredible feeling, to know you are again becoming a full part of the universe and will soon be whole instead of separated as we are when we are in between youth and old age. I may sound like I am losing my senses. I am not. Never fear. My mind is as sharp as ever. Perhaps it is sharper, in order to feel what I have not before.

As for Miss Laerty, I have sent a short note to her, an agreement to your request that she should ask for any assistance she may require that I may have the ability to do. I have a good roof and plenty of sustenance, if not much more. She is welcome, with the child if need be. In truth, I would enjoy holding newness in my arms again even if it is not part of you and of myself.

I should explain not keeping up with the place, so you will not be surprised at its decline. The Terry boys young Cameron asked to check in on me and help out have declined to do so. I believe there is some belief that Cameron may have covered for you with Miss Monroe and have decided to separate themselves from us because of it. It is beyond me how they would believe as much, but I respect their feelings and will not impose myself as a burden to anyone. I did hope to have it in its best shape for your homecoming. I shall have to settle for what I can do.

This letter is far too long and perhaps you will not appreciate my sending it at all, considering your thoughts on the matter. However, I could not keep from writing and if you have changed your mind, I would not dare disappoint you.

Know, my dear Abraham, you are the center of my heart and I never stop thinking of you. I dearly look forward to your return, and if that is not to happen, then we shall meet soon in a better place.

With love, your very proud father,
Charles Luchner

Abe captured a deep breath and fought moisture in his eyes. This was one reason he did not want to exchange letters with his father. It made the urge to work at his side each day and talk on the front porch at night after dinner much stronger than when he could block it from his thoughts.

Cameron's brothers were not helping or looking after him. He was alone. The thought pushed him off his cot to pace the tent. Out away from town on his own. Abe didn't worry about his safety as far as intruders. No one in town was a better shot. That would be of no help if he fell or had medical needs unexpectedly.

"What's wrong, Abe? Which letter do you carry while you pace?"

He turned to Cameron. "My father's."

His friend came close, studying him. "Is he not well?"

"Yes, he seems well."

"Then what worries you?"

Abe shook his head. There was no use infuriating Cameron even further with his family. And there was nothing he could do.

"You are not going to hide it from me." Cam grabbed the papers from Abe's hand before he could stop him.

"You don't want to read that. Give it to me." Abe tried to reach around his friend, but Cameron wouldn't give in.

"Ha, did you think I would be surprised your father would not believe the child was yours but has no trouble believing it's mine?"

"That's enough. Give it to me."

Cam turned with a stare. "Since when do we hide things from each other?"

Abe couldn't argue. Even if Cameron would be more angry with his family, Abe couldn't refuse his knowing. "Read it then. I was only trying to spare you." He went over and plopped on his bunk, wishing for his mattress and his plump pillow and his soft … no, he wouldn't let his mind go there. He would not.

"The insufferable, ungrateful wretches!" Cam tossed the letter on Abe's bunk. "They are going against their word because of the child? What does it have to do with your father? He is not to blame. Wait until I get hold of their scrawny necks!" With a quick breath to control himself, he eyed Abe. "And you were not going to tell me."

"What is the point? Now you are even angrier and there is nothing can be done from here."

"Isn't there? I think there is." Cam paced back to his bunk and grabbed paper and pen.

"What are you doing?"

"Rewriting my will."

Abe bolted to his feet. "Cam, you're angry now. You should not make such hasty decisions while you are angry."

"Angry. I am well beyond angry. They owe me more respect. I have overlooked it time and again, but this I will not overlook. Those do-nothing, worthless, spoiled boys will get nothing that belongs to me."

Abe shrugged. "Of course. It should go to your child."

Cam looked up as though the thought hadn't crossed his mind. "My child. Yes. The child with no name. How am I to put her in my will?" He looked over at Abe's stand. "And what did Maura have to say? Did she tell you the child's name?"

Abe was shocked to realize he'd forgotten Maura's letter.

"You haven't read it?"

"No."

A light amusement crossed his friend's face. "Well then, perhaps you should, so I can name my child in my will. And Abe … I am naming you, as well."

"Me? Whatever for?"

"My stipend that comes from my part of the family inheritance shall go to my child, and to whoever raises my child should I be unable. I wish that to be you. I have no right to ask this, but if I do not go home, I want you to be my child's father. And be sure he knows of me, only the good parts, you hear."

A father? To Cameron's child? "And if I do not go home, either?"

Cam's face fell. Then he raised it and nodded. "You, my friend, will go home. If none of the rest of us do, you will. I know. You are meant for great things. This will not be your last stand."

"As much as I appreciate the confidence, what if you name me and I do not?"

He stood again and wandered a moment, head down, lips in a thoughtful frown. Then he stopped. "In that case, I will leave everything to Maura. Would that be improper?"

"I am sure she would be better than either of us as a parent."

Cam chuckled. "You are surely right. Then it's settled. Open the letter and tell me the name of my child."

Abe felt better reading the letter now that he had his friend's blessing and request. Again, he was sure not to cut anything but the top seam, although he knew Cam grew impatient. The letter this time had a different smell. Hers. But also … newness, as his father called it. He could smell the baby on the sheets of paper? No. He had to be imagining it. The letter from his father had him too thrown.

"Are you going to read it or only hold it?" Cam threw an amused expression. "Why do I think Maura's charms have begun to rub off on you, my friend?"

"What?" Abe tried to not realize what he meant. Although he did. "You know how I feel about letters from home. Two in one day … it's only that. The reminder of home I do not wish to have."

"And still, I don't understand. It makes it easier to do what we're doing, does it not? The reminder of home is the only thing most days that keeps me going, not that I have much of a home of which to return, other than my child. I suppose if not for her, I would have nothing."

"I am nothing all of a sudden?"

"You continue to say you will not go home."

"And you continue to say I will. So then you have two of us who will be glad to have you home, at least. And I am sure Maura will be, as well." At his mention of her name, Abraham looked down at the sheets and unfolded them. He didn't wish to read it to Cameron, especially as she had written three full pages and he was tired of talking.

"Take the strain out of your face." Cameron threw a pair of rolled-up socks at him. "I do not want to hear everything, Abe. Only skim through and tell me the name and then read at your leisure. I have a will to write."

He hoped he didn't look as relieved as he was. And he didn't have to skim. It was nearly the first thing she said and he read it aloud:

As to Cameron wondering about the child's name, she does not have one and I meant to mention it in my last letter. I was too distraught, and apologize for being so. Sadie was still deciding on the name when … when she left the child as she didn't expect. It is of urgent importance that Cameron name his daughter first, and also send immediately a letter to show I am to keep the child until his return. The home tells me I cannot since there is no one with a legal claim on her. They mean to adopt her out. Sadie begged me not to allow it to happen. Please, I will hold them off, but an urgent response is required. I cannot allow Miss Terry to go to a stranger. I cannot. If need be, I will flee and hide away until such time as Cameron either makes his intentions clear or until he comes home and I can hand the child into his arms. I will do this without regret but with fear I will not be able to hide well enough.

Abe looked at his friend.

Cam nodded. "The will, and the letter for Maura to be guardian until my return. Both tonight. Bless her soul. I will never be able to repay her kindness."

Unsure he should say what crossed his mind, Abe said it anyway. "I think she has grown attached to the child, too much to lose her. You will repay her by allowing her to see the baby often, as is only fair and decent."

"Yes. Of course. Perhaps she could continue to keep the child during the day while I work."

Abe watched his thoughtful nod and remained silent, as Cam went to his writing immediately. He was glad for the time to read the rest of her words. She spoke of home, of the canyon and the color of the mountains and 'the home' she had returned to – for sake of the soldiers, not for the administrators, with whom she was still angry. She had to deny her anger while there, to placate those who thought the baby should be taken from her. Being pleasant sometimes taxed all her strength and she found herself leaving early, much too early.

Yet, she had taken his advice and hired two girls to help around the house, to cook and clean, and a well-trained young man to help teach Rudy how to care for the garden. He was happy to hear it. She spoke of what her garden was growing, on how well it was doing with such expert hands to tend it. Better than her own, she said. As much as she enjoyed the work of it as she could, she never learned how to grow vegetables large and healthy as most did. This summer, they had a good crop of tomatoes, which Rudy adored. She had found him more than once picking one straight from the garden and eating it as though it were an apple. It had made her laugh. Abe wished he could have seen it. But in a way, he did, her descriptions were so vivid.

She also mentioned a note from his father, overly grateful for the small gesture, both to Abraham and to his father. She'd taken the time the same night to write a return note, and she'd sent Rudy with Mr. Weathers out to Abraham's huouse to check in on his father and to do what he could to help. If he didn't object, she might go herself in time, but not if it would offend Abraham in any way. She missed her father, and visiting his would be a comfort, she said.

He wanted to reply tonight, to write a long letter in return, to tell her how honored he was she would visit his father when it was convenient. He would not so soon. Cameron was writing her tonight. His letter was urgent. Abe's was not. And he needed to think on it before he reacted. Her words had touched him too deeply. He had to find distance before he allowed himself to answer.

Cameron set one paper aside and picked up the next.

"So what did you name her?"

"Her name will be Samantha Louise. Samantha, from Sadie and Cam, Louise Terry."

Samantha Louise. Also, Abe presumed, after his middle name of Louis. "The name of a lady. I hope I shall be able to return home with you to meet her and watch her grow into one."

"You'd best do just that, my friend."

seventeen

Maura clenched her upper lip in her teeth. Cameron named her both temporary guardian of Samantha Louise, a name she was instantly in love with, and permanent guardian in case neither he nor Abe returned. As well as guardian of all funds that would belong to his daughter. It was high praise, an honor. And yet, she was only second in line for the child. He made Abraham the first.

Tears came to her eyes but she promptly pushed them away. It was unfair. She was the one who took care of Sadie, the one who delivered the baby, the one who took care of her and fought for her. Why should Abraham take custody in case … but it wouldn't matter. Cameron would come home and raise his daughter. He'd also assured her visits as often as she liked.

There was something of a hint in the way he worded it, as though the offer was for more than visits to the child. Maybe she was imagining. Cameron had moved on from thinking of her in that manner, had he not? He was devastated over Sadie's loss. But then … there was a tone.

Well, she would have to deal with that bridge as she came upon it. She had her letter, the one that proved she was to keep the child. Maura wouldn't hesitate to take it to the county office and file it, along with Cameron's will he asked her to take at the same time. Both were witnessed and signed by his company commander. They could not be denied or refused.

+_+_+

"Rudy, put your sister in her stroller, please." Maura grinned at the way the boy jumped up and went to carefully take Samantha from her cradle. He talked to her as he picked her up and kept talking as he laid her in the stroller.

"Are we going to the home today?"

"No, we're going on an adventure. What do you think of that?"

"An adventure? What kind of adventure?"

"You'll see when we get there. I think we all deserve one by now. Don't you?"

The boy nodded and eyed her.

"What is it?" Maura noted a question.

"Is Mr. Weathers taking us?"

"No. This is a walking adventure. Only you and Samantha and I. Think you can keep up?" She grinned.

"Yes, but Miss Maura, shouldn't we ask Mr. Weathers..."

"Mr. Weathers is too old to walk far."

"Then someone else? Someone strong and ... and..."

"What is bothering you, Rudy?"

He frowned, remaining silent until Maura approached and set her hands on his shoulders. "Town is dangerous now with all the strangers coming in, not like it used to be. I know about what happened to Miss..."

"Oh, honey, the man who attacked Miss Jill was caught and put away. It doesn't mean it's no longer safe. Besides, I have you at my side." She leaned down to kiss his head.

"But Miss Maura, I'm not very big yet. My friends my age are all bigger, the ones I have. Maybe they can come with us? I'll run ask."

"Rudy." Maura had to grab his shirt back to keep him from bolting. "Why are you so upset? It was once and Miss Jill was out after dark by herself. It is bright daylight now and many will be out wandering, those we know."

He dropped his head, averting his gaze.

"What is it you do not wish to tell me? Come on. Spill."

His shoulders rose and fell. "Some in town ... well, they ..."

"They what?"

He popped his head up. "They say things about you, Miss Maura. Because of Samantha. Because Miss Sadie stayed with us. They think that maybe you didn't want Miss Sadie to live because ... because you and Mr. Cameron..."

Maura crouched to see him better. "I know what they say. We both know they are wrong. I loved Sadie as a sister. Why does it matter what they say? No one else cared enough about her to come to her assistance. Let them say as they please."

"But ... but they think you and Mr. Cameron were..." He shook his head. "I can't say it. But they won't help if you need. No one will come if we call for help. My friends will. The ones who still talk to me even if I stay with you where everyone says I don't belong."

She pulled him into a tight hug. "You know what? We don't need their help, do we? We're managing on our own." She looked over at Samantha's fuss. "And I want you to know, if it matters to you, that Mr. Cameron and I were friends. He did ask to court me, but it was no more than that. Nothing improper. So when they say those things, you keep your chin up and know the truth matters more than what they think."

"I'll challenge anyone I hear say it again. Even if I'm not big, I..."

"You'll do no such thing." She stopped an argument she saw on his face. "Listen to me close now. Your safety is more important." Maura tapped a finger against his chest. "This is what matters. Right? Sadie held more feeling in her heart for Cameron than many people do for those they're married to. That makes it right, and she would have married him when he returned. In her heart, she was married to him. That's what matters. People have some foolish ideas sometimes, but it doesn't mean they're right. So never mind what they say. Keep your chin up, look them in the eye, and then walk away knowing the truth. They'll see they're wrong and you won't have to say a word. Will you do that for me?"

He frowned. "I would rather challenge them."

Maura gave him a grin and scuffed his hair. "I know you would, and I'm proud you wish to fight for my honor. There could be a day come I will be happy to accept it, but only after I know you can defend yourself well. I will not have you hurt for me. That would break my heart. Nothing is worse than that. Remember, Rudy. Nothing matters more than protecting what's in your heart."

With a small nod, he sighed and looked over at Samantha's continued fuss. "Still, I would feel better if some of my friends could go on the adventure with us."

"Well then, run see if they will. But we're leaving in a few minutes."

Checking every lock in the house for the third time after closing themselves behind it, Maura reigned in her emotions that threatened to spill over the brim. Rudy was right. A transient taking advantage of free sustenance at the home had followed them out to the pond at the edge of town. The boys played in the water as Maura sat along the top of the hill and watched over them, baby in her arms, when the man appeared, a horrid leer in his eyes and words spoken she would never repeat. She had no idea how he followed without her knowing. Or maybe he'd lingered near the pond behind the spread of trees to one side. He must have. The group of boys running up from the pond when Maura yelled to Rudy startled him enough to change his mind.

She apparently wasn't worth the trouble of fighting off four strong boys.

She hadn't let them see how shaken she was. She was the adult and had to get them all home again. With every step, she prayed he wouldn't return. Even once home with doors locked, Rudy would not leave her side. That is until she insisted she needed a bath once the baby fell asleep. He paced around the house and kept watch. He said he would and Maura didn't argue since it would be no use. He had finally worn himself out and she sent him off to bed with assurance all doors and windows were locked.

They stopped and filed a report, but Rudy was right about that, too. The officer looked her up and down, looked at the baby and at Rudy, and took little info. They would do nothing. Maura knew they would do nothing. Never mind her papa had been well respected in town and had helped it grow with his money. He was gone now. So was their loyalty to him.

eighteen

She would go crazy if she didn't go out. Maura knew she would. She wanted to go to the canyon, stare out over Snake River, let her eyes wander to the shadowed mountains. She hadn't been up to the mountains in years, not since her mother was still alive. Her mother had loved them so, taking the long drive up part way and camping overnight in the noise of the crickets and owls and an occasional wolf howl. If she closed her eyes, Maura could almost be there again, with the cool fresh evening air wisping along her cheeks and leaves rustling above. No other human anywhere they could see or hear. She wanted that now nearly more than she could stand.

Out. She had to go out. But she hadn't been past the middle of town since that day. It was silly, she decided. That man had to be far away by now. Even if nothing would be done, he wouldn't know that. He would have high-tailed it out of there instead of taking the chance.

Forcing steel from somewhere inside she thought she had lost, Maura called to Rudy and asked him to see if the Weathers would like to go to the canyon with them. There was no one else to ask. No one else still spoke to Maura, other than a few she worked with at the home whenever she made herself go. She didn't want to be there. Between the leers of the men and the whispers of the women and her administrators suggesting some man or other who needed a wife to care for him, it tore into her soul too much. She was only comfortable at home, her father's home, with the doors and windows locked. She would, at times, open the upper windows to let in fresh air, but never the bottom.

"Miss Maura!" Rudy stormed in, mail in hand. "Mail's here already. And the Weathers would love to go to the canyon. They say they're glad you're getting out again. They're worried if you're all right. There's a letter from Mr. Cameron, and a letter from Mr. Abraham."

"What? From both?" She frowned as she accepted the mail, and set the rest aside. No wonder everyone talked, with both Cameron and Abraham writing her. She supposed she should ask one of them to stop. But whom? She could never refuse Cameron, since she had care of his daughter. But Abraham ... Maura so enjoyed his letters. No. They could think what they pleased. She would ask neither to stop.

    Grasping blank paper and pen, she tucked them into her carry case along with the letters and readied the baby to go out.

    It was longer than she wished before she had a chance to read them. Susanne Weathers was highly talkative, unusual, and Maura didn't dare be rude after they were so nice to accompany her. They talked too much of the incident until Maura assured them she was past it and ready to let it out of her mind.

    When Mr. Weathers settled down to rest his eyes in the late June sun, Susanne asked if Maura would mind if she pulled out a novel to continue, as she was very into the story and wanted to get to the end. Maura didn't mind at all. She picked up an extra blanket to move to the deep grass close to the edge of the canyon, allowed Rudy and Tony to spread it for her as she warned them not to get too close to the edge, and laid Samantha on her stomach so she could work on building her tiny arm muscles. She propped her parasol to keep the sun off the baby and allowed it to fall squarely on her own head.

    Maura opened Cameron's letter first.

Dearest Maura,

    I received a distressing note today from my youngest brother who has decided not to write me off, after all. I am, as you can guess, unsure of his intentions but if what he says is true, I am doubly – nay, triply – ashamed I am not there taking care of matters as I should be. He tells me the townsfolk have cast you aside for the simple reason that you are caring for my "bastard" child, who they do not believe is mine. I hear, as well, there was an incident that young Rudy and his friends were able to manage. Please tell me this is only a way to make me wish again I had never agreed to come to this truly God-forsaken place and not truth. I should be devastated if I have caused you more harm yet.

    If it is, and if there is anything I can do to help correct the misunderstanding, more than the note I signed stating the child is my own, please tell me. I am at your will to do anything I can.

    I thank you again for your graciousness and loving care of Samantha, as well as for taking the extra time to write and let me know everything she is doing. My eyes fill even now thinking of what I miss and how much more I shall miss until this is over.

    They say it will be soon. I no longer dare believe it since they have said it so often. Do not fret. Abe and I are still watching each other's backs and plan to be glued together all the way back home.

You will know him well enough by then through his letters I insist he continue writing and I hope we will all be friends. I do wish him to be as an uncle to my child, considering my brothers are uninterested. Save the youngest. And, as I said, I am unsure of that truth. We shall see.

My back is in much pain tonight so I am afraid I must leave you with a short letter. My friend Abraham will, I am sure, make up for it. He is in a jolly mood for some unknown reason. It must bring him joy to see me in pain. I am, of course, teasing. At this moment, he yells at me to lie down and rest. I tell him it does no good any longer. He continues to believe it will, or at least that it will be well once we are home and I no longer have this ruck over my shoulders.

My best wishes,
Cameron

P.S. Please do be careful. I could not live with myself if anything at all should happen to you. Give my heartfelt thanks to young Rudy and tell him I very much look forward to meeting him.

She would not cry. Maura would not permit the Weathers to see her cry. His brother told him. She wished he hadn't, even if he did mean well. She wasn't so sure of that, either. The boy – she shouldn't call him a boy, she supposed, as he was seventeen – had thrown her a light nod when they ran across each other in town, with a long gaze at the baby. Maybe he did mean well. Maybe she had one ally left in town, other than her neighbors. Mr. Weathers was getting on in years. Susanne's husband was due home soon and so she and Tony would head back out to the country. Susanne talked of taking her father with. That debate seemed unsettled.

Picking up Abraham's letter, she set it down again. She would answer Cameron first. She would assure him he should not worry and what others thought was not her concern. After doing so, her words kept flowing onto the paper, as they had when he first left, when she hadn't known about Sadie, when they were still friends and he was her confidante. She needed it. There was nothing he could do for her from there, except allow her to ramble and understand how she needed to ramble.

Maybe there was something he could do. At the end of the letter, she considered asking if he would still promise his hand to her. She was an outsider already. What difference would it make if she took him back now? Samantha needed both mother and father, and she couldn't bear the thought of letting her go. She also couldn't bear the thought of always being alone. She was tired of being alone, of having no one but the children and two neighbors who would desert her. Nothing but the big house she had to pay for help to care for.

At the end of the too-long letter in which she couldn't quite make herself ask for his hand, Maura gathered her things and the blanket and told Rudy they must leave. Dusk descended and made the air cool. She hadn't meant to stay out so late. She wondered that the Weathers hadn't mentioned it.

With apologies, Maura helped them carry their folding chairs to the car. The design on the wide top slat caught her eye. She'd noticed it before but hadn't paid it any attention. There was a certain familiarity about it, however, and she ran her fingers across the carved landscape.

"Ah, you admire fine artwork, I see." Mr. Weathers set a hand on her arm. "Have you seen his work beyond that in the bank?"

"His?"

"Young Mr. Luchner did these for me some time ago."

"Oh." She studied the precise depiction of a blacksmith at work.

"They were a gift, to be honest, from your Mr. Terry." He paused long enough to catch her eyes. "He's a fiery soul, that one. Always into trouble. Nothing of much consequence, only enough to set his parents to yelling and withholding allowance. I saved him from their knowledge one of his shenanigans just after they moved to town. He was grateful enough to have his new friend carve these for me. My father was a blacksmith. I feel his presence as I use them." He shook his head as he admired the work. "A huge return for such a little favor. The boy has a good heart and a mighty generous streak."

A good heart. Yes, Maura, no matter what else she might say of Cameron, would never argue that. And generous. She felt it was a hint from Mr. Weathers that she possibly should have included the question of a proposal in the letter. A man with a good heart and the ability to remain mother to the children she loved: what more did she truly need? Passion wasn't an absolute necessity, was it? It was hard for her to answer, since she had never felt it.

Perhaps, in return for care of his daughter and Sadie, Maura would ask Cameron to hire Abe to carve chairs for her, as well, for when she was old enough she wouldn't want to sit on the ground when she went out. A huge return for such a little favor.

The first thing Maura did upon arriving home was to leave the baby in Rudy's care and walk around to check everything: windows, rooms, closets. She turned on more lights than normal and scolded herself for doing so. She had to return to her senses. Which meant returning to work, and to shopping on her own instead of always sending one of the girls. She enjoyed shopping, milling around the fresh fruits and vegetables and cuts of fish and beef to choose which she wanted. Her vegetable garden was coming along much better now that someone else was caring for it … and perhaps Samantha and Rudy would be the same: better under another woman's care. She was getting entirely too jumpy. It wasn't good for them. Maura knew it wasn't.

They needed more calm, more control. They needed what she used to be.

With a deep breath, she returned to the children and took them into the kitchen. They would have sandwiches for supper, as they were out so late. Rudy enjoyed slicing the meat for them while Maura cut up tomatoes and lettuce and sliced the cheese off the block. The normalcy of it soothed her. As did talking with Samantha as the baby lay in the half-reclined seat Maura perched on the counter.

While they ate, she remembered Abraham's letter. She'd not yet read it. She wanted to do as she had done as a young girl so often: rush through dinner to run up to her room and secretly read the note she'd been passed earlier in the day from the boy down the road. Their clandestine 'affair' had lasted quite some time, eight full months, before he moved away and she was crushed. His promise to write had never been fulfilled.

What a long time ago, and still she wondered how he was, if he was well, what he had done with his adulthood so far. Perhaps he was overseas, also. Maybe he hadn't come home. Or wouldn't. Or he hadn't gone because … of his urgent business needed at home or for medical reasons or … or maybe she didn't want to know.

Maura took a long swallow of iced tea with a splash of fresh lemon and asked Rudy if he was finished. The boy was nearly asleep at the table and simply nodded.

"Go clean up and get ready for bed, then, while I take care of this."

"It's too early for bed."

"Yes, but it's not too early to be ready. After the day's adventure, I believe we could all settle in sooner than usual, don't you agree?"

"But I'm not tired."

She gave him a grin and stroked his hair. "Get ready, anyway. I'll read you a story after." That was enough to send the boy scampering. He loved to be read to. Maura could hardly make herself do it. She detested reading aloud. She hoped Cameron would enjoy it more.

Cameron.

She knew there was a tone in his voice, even with only paper and ink, that should not be there. Although, why shouldn't there? It would be a nice solution. Even if she didn't love him in that manner, she could learn. And she would have the children.

Follow your heart. Her father's words echoed in her mind. But he was gone. He'd left her alone to deal with all of this on her own. If Father had been at the pond, that man wouldn't have considered threatening her. Even if he was old. He was a good shot and he went nowhere without his weapon. The whole town knew it. It that man didn't, he soon would have.

Maybe that's what Maura needed. She should pull out her father's pistol and learn to use it. But how would she learn? No one would teach her. And she didn't want to be taught. She'd seen enough of the results to not want to cause them. Except maybe she would, if someone threatened her again, or worse, if they threatened the children. She would, then. But who would teach her? Could she figure it out on her own?

With the table cleared and wiped and dishes cleaned and put away, she noted the baby's head tilting to its side in near slumber. Yes, it had been a long day for all of them. Early to bed tonight.

Settled beneath her blankets, propped up with the pillows behind her back, Maura carefully tore the letter open. She should have read it before bed, she supposed, but she was tired, as well. Stretching her legs out beneath the covers seemed a prerequisite for relaxing with Abe's words. Abraham's. She had no right to shorten his name as though they were familiar.

She set the envelope aside and stared at the papers. Familiar. Something about the sound of it in her head startled her, warmed her. Familiar with Abraham. The thought of it felt more right than Cameron ever had. She noted a light rise of the corners of her mouth. Familiar with Abraham. Perhaps.

A stir in her stomach caused her to snap open the letter, too anxious to devour his words to be patient any longer. First, she brought it to her nose and sniffed the odd smell. It wasn't so odd this time. It was … familiar. She grinned again.

Dear Miss Laerty,

As our friend Cameron is rather incapacitated tonight – although he insists on writing you a quick note while I yell at him to lie down – he asks that I take over and fill you in on recent events, as well as emphasize…

One thing at a time is best, I suppose.

We appear to be close to the end of this journey. In that, although I cannot say much in a letter, I mean Samantha's father should soon be able to take her off your too-full hands and ease your burden. Although you try to hide it in your letters, I hear tension in your tone and if I had enough power with my new rank – did Cameron mention I was promoted to Sergeant? – I would send him home to you immediately. That is, to his daughter, to decrease your burden. I am glad to hear you hired girls to help with the house and garden. I should tell you Cameron could also take care of that when he is home in return for all you have done for him, but alas, you shall still need to hire the girls for both tasks, house and garden, as Cam is, I'm terribly afraid, a horrible slob inside and wouldn't know a turnip from a potato in the garden. If the neighbors would not make assumptions, I would be more than glad to help with the garden, as our farm is actually a farm which grows living things of our own hands, not a farm marked as such when hardly anything but hay and troublemakers grow on it…

I had a brief interference. Cam decided to look over my shoulder to see what I wrote you and is arguing against being a troublemaker. Perhaps he is right. My apologies. The only trouble he has made here has been to himself, as is normal. He has become a dependable soldier and yet does so look forward to seeing his daughter and learning what a father needs to learn. I do wish he and his own father were closer to make that task easier. However, he has spent much time at my home – oh, how that word sinks into my heart deeply – and around my father and he has seen what a good father should be.

My apologies, again, dear Maura, as you are in all likelihood still mourning your own father. I know little of the man and do hope you had a good relationship, as well. Tell me of him, if you wish. I am always glad to listen. Or ignore that request if it makes it harder.

I, myself, have started writing my father, although I said I would not, with the thought it would be easier on him to adjust to my possible permanent absence if he grew used to my temporary absence without my constant interruptions to tell him I am still around. I find I can no longer protect him in that way as I wished. To remain so unselfish out here is nigh impossible, I'm afraid. As such, I hope you will forgive my rambling to you in this manner, as well.

I should burn this and start over.

As I was about to do so, Cam stopped me. I asked him to read it and tell me then if I should not burn it. He refused both, assuring me anything I wrote you would be all right. I am not so sure.

But still, here I keep writing. Nothing but nonsense. Saying not much of anything just to say something. Thank you for your patience if you are still reading. If you are not, then it doesn't matter what I write, I suppose.

Cameron told me of his brother's letter. It stilled my heart as it did his to imagine what near trouble you were in. I would like to repeat my offer to go to my father for assistance. There is space for you and the two children. No intruder dare go near as handy as my father is with a rifle, and with the dog warning of anyone's approach. You would all be quite safe and my father would enjoy the company.

I understand if you are concerned what others would say of that arrangement. Please, do not worry for my sake, if you are, or for my father's. We have never bothered with that nonsense and would not do so now.

I'm afraid I skipped ahead of the topic again. It is too much foremost on my mind not to ... and I again say too much. You are, I feel, like family to me almost because of your friendship with Cam and because of mine with him that is also very deep. Therefore, I forget myself, and pray you will not think unkindly of me for doing so.

Like family. Did he mean like a sister or cousin? Maura set the letter on her night stand with a thunk of her fingers against the wood. Like family. How dare he suppose such a thing? They had never even met. That was why he was so kind, so personal. He expected her to marry Cameron, she supposed, simply because she cared for his child. His children. Rudy would stay with Samantha. Cam had already agreed to take him as a son. It did not, in any way, mean Maura had to accept Cameron, simply because she loved his children.

Samantha was more hers…

She turned to her side away from the stand holding the letter. A sister or cousin? Her heart sank.

But why should it? What was wrong with her? They hadn't even met. She had only seen him from a distance. Had only … admired him from a distance. Not only his fine figure, strong straight shoulders, wavy hair, but also the table at the bank she admired each time she was there. And the other carvings she had seen in the houses of the families her father visited. She detested the socializing but adored the carvings and hearing about how they had been requested.

Abraham. The artist, farmer, soldier. The romantic. She did know him. Well enough. As well as she knew Cameron, to be truthful, since Cameron hid so much of himself when they were together. Abe didn't. Abraham.

With a sigh, she propped herself up again and retrieved the letter, skimming to where she had left off.

> *… and pray you will not think unkindly of me for doing so.*
> *Back to the first subject, since I drifted much too far away from it, we have come to a pivotal juncture and tomorrow should tell us whether our hopes of leaving soon were too high. It could be a hard day, or a celebratory day. There is the possibility of both, I suppose. I tell myself I should wait until after tomorrow to write this so you do not have to wonder which it was, but I would suppose any news of that importance shall arrive long before my letter and this will be anticlimactic. We can only hope.*
> *Since my news is now finished, I should end this. However, Cam is deep asleep and I am still very much awake and wish for your company however I can get it. I cannot tell you how much I admire your descriptions of your activities, of the life around you. I will try now to return the favor and describe our surroundings and typical days, leaving out the more vulgar things of which you would not enjoy hearing, of which none of us enjoy seeing or even knowing…*

Rubbing her eyes, Maura finally set the letter back on the night stand. It was quite the long letter: a good thing she did not try to read it at the canyon. The description, Abraham's description, was so much more beautiful than hers. She saw it well enough to allow a few tears for him, for Cameron, for all the boys over there so far from home. She could scarcely imagine living in that manner. It made her petty troubles more petty. It made her feel insufferable for whining so about what she dealt with. There would be no more of it.

And she would not run to Abe's father like a frightened child. Perhaps she would visit and be sure he didn't need assistance. Rudy and an older boy had gone a week before, had stayed to visit and came back with fresh blueberries they picked from the vines with Abe's father's help. He had welcomed them back any time. Maura was invited, also.

Perhaps she would.

nineteen

Mr. Weathers said he had been glad to drive out to see his old friend, Charles Luchner. His grandson went, as well, as company for Rudy. The boy's mother enjoyed the time alone as she could find it. Alone. A word Maura began to detest.

She sighed as town approached.

"Are you tired, dear?" Mr. Weathers glanced over. "Did we keep you too long with our chatting?"

"No, not at all. That is, yes, I am tired but I enjoyed the conversation. Mr. Luchner is a lovely man."

"Ah, as is his son. You are acquainted, though, I believe?"

"No. That is, not in person. Cameron … Mr. Terry and he are good friends and I have heard about him."

"And the letters that come to you from Abraham?"

Maura felt her face warm.

"My apologies. I don't mean to pry."

"Yes, he does write at times. Cameron is not much of a writer and has injured his back and so lies flat on his cot when he is not working. It is hard for him to write but he does want to hear about his children."

A half grin accompanied a half nod. He didn't quite believe how casual she made it sound. But it was. There was nothing more to it. She looked back to check on the baby asleep in her brother's arms. It would be hard to get her to sleep at a decent time if she didn't wake soon. And Maura was tired. But then, it was nothing compared to what Abraham was dealing with. And Cameron.

"Here we are. Oh."

The start in Mr. Weathers's voice made Maura turn back. They were nearly in front of her house. The front door was open. As they grew closer, she also saw windows smashed.

"What happened?" Rudy, from the back.

Maura couldn't answer. She couldn't react. She sat in the car looking at her house. Invaded. Robbed, most likely.

"Stay in the car, dear. We'll run bring the sheriff to check it before we go in." With another look at the house, Mr. Weathers turned the car around and went back to the middle of town.

"Can you see what's missing?"

Maura ambled through the mess of overturned chairs and emptied drawers. It didn't seem anything was gone, only scattered. Thrown. As in a rampage. She shook her head as she walked. Rudy and Samantha were next door with Susanne, safely tucked inside. Maura didn't want them in the house. She didn't want to be in the house. Nearly numb, she went to the small safe in her father's room upstairs. Untouched. So were her mother's jewels, other than on the floor, scattered. They were still there.

She went to her room next. It was perfectly neat, as she'd left it. She opened drawers. Everything was there, untouched ... except her letters. Abraham's letters. And Cameron's. Someone had taken them from her night stand drawer.

Why?

She sank onto her bed and stared at the empty drawer. Why the letters? Why every room a mess with nothing touched except hers that was neat with the missing letters?

"Miss Laerty?" The sheriff stood at her doorway. He would not enter the room with her in it alone. "Have you found anything missing?"

How could she answer? Should she admit what was gone? It would only bring consternation. The town already looked down on her because of her relations with the two friends. She shook her head.

"Do you know what they might have been looking for?"

She shook her head again. The truth this time. What did they hope to find in the words of two soldiers away from home?

"Well then, I'll send someone to patch up your windows for safety until you can have them fixed. Do you have someone to stay with you, and to help with this mess?"

"No." There was no one. She would deal with it, as she did everything else, by herself.

Maura pulled the afghan over her shoulders and tried not to get too comfortable on the chaise. She would not go up to her room tonight. She and Rudy had straightened the front rooms enough to be presentable and the rest would wait until morning. She nearly didn't get the boy to go on up to bed when she asked. He was afraid. So she walked with him, tucked him in and kissed his forehead to tell him all was fine, and crept back down the stairs to keep watch. The windows were boarded enough to prevent a body getting through, and Maura had tacked pieces of material around the inside to keep the mosquitoes out, as well. She watched now as the edges flapped in a light breeze.

Her thoughts remained with wondering why anyone would do such a thing and why they wanted the letters. A jilted lover, perhaps? Was there someone who wanted Abraham's attentions before he left and hoped to regain them when he returned? Perhaps Cameron had another girl on the side who.... No, she wouldn't allow herself to believe such a thing. And even so, why bother her about it? Maura had given no one any indication that she wanted either of them.

But who else then? It had to be … except there was too much damage done too quickly to be a single woman. It looked more the mess of at least two or three men. Perhaps some who had protested the home, and yet, she was hardly there now. Why bother her and not the administrators?

Her eyes closed against her will. She shoved them open again. What she would do if the prowlers returned, she wasn't sure, but she had to at least be aware.

A thought crossed her mind. Her father's pistol. Even if she didn't know how to use it, an intruder wouldn't be sure she didn't. At least it would give her a chance. She should have agreed to stay with the Weathers as they asked. Foolish. So very foolish to be so prideful.

+_+_+

She woke to a tapping. As she jumped the pistol fell onto the floor with a thunk and she retrieved it quickly. The noise came from the door. Bits of light seeped through cracks between the wood planks over the windows.

Maura made her way over and looked out the only window not broken, the thin pane beside the door. Abraham's father. The thought of why he was there scared her more than any prowler would have. Something happened. To Abraham.

Gathering herself, she shoved the pistol into a nearby drawer and returned to let him in.

Mr. Luchner gave her a polite nod. "Miss Laerty, please forgive the intrusion without notice."

"Not at all. Please. Come in."

He eyed her a moment before another nod prompted him to follow. He glanced around at the parts of mess she and Rudy had been too tired to clean.

"Forgive the state of the parlor. I'm afraid we've…"

"Yes, I heard. Do you know who it was?"

"No." She fought back emotion. It wasn't the time. "Is everything all right?" Catching herself, she stepped back. "I'm sorry. That was abrupt. Would you like … I overslept but I'll make coffee." Maura didn't bother to see if he would follow. She escaped into the mess of the kitchen, bit her lip a moment, then scrimmaged through to find what she needed.

Mr. Luchner did follow and she asked him to take a chair. Instead, he bent to pick something off the floor and replace it on a shelf. And continued.

"No, please." Maura hurried over. "Rudy and I will manage. And the girls I've hired. They should be here soon. I am surprised they aren't already…"

"They will not come back." He caught her eyes. "Miss Laerty, you should sit a moment."

"What is it?"

"Please." He held a chair for her and she couldn't refuse. Something had happened to Abe. He wasn't coming back. She could feel it…

The elder man took a chair himself and faced her. "I will apologize beforehand for being blunt, but I am afraid I must be."

She nodded enough to tell him the apology wasn't necessary.

"Are you betrothed to Mr. Terry as some say?"

"Betrothed? Why, no. Who would still say I am?"

"Many." He paused with a slight tilt of his head. "You had no intention, then, of being so?"

Maura started to shake her head and stopped. Perhaps. Perhaps part of her did. He wouldn't turn her away as any other decent man would now. She could stay with the children…

"Ask your heart. That is what I want to know. Did you intend, in your heart, to be his betrothed?"

"No." She couldn't stop the moisture in her eyes and wiped at them. "No. I may have little option, although I have thought of leaving, of going somewhere, anywhere but here. Except the children. I cannot leave the children. They are too much like my own now. I would miss them so. Cameron promises I can still see them. It might be best, if we … considering all things…"

"Cameron will not be returning."

Her eyes flashed to his. "What?"

"I believe that's what your break in was about. His brothers, I suspect. When they heard about his loss yesterday, they went straight in to claim his…"

"Wait." She shook her head. "It can't be. He has children. His daughter. He's coming back for them. He looks forward to being a father…"

Kindness and sorry reflected in his eyes as he took her fingers in his. "I am sorry. I came early to be the one to tell you. He was lost in battle. They say he died a hero, saving other lives. Turns out he was a better man than I ever expected. I worried about Abraham running with him…"

Maura wiped at tears. "No. Not Cameron." She tried to steady herself. "And Abraham?" Her voice shook. "He was always at Cameron's side. I know he was. So they're both…"

"No. Abe is alive. Injured. Not badly as I hear. Hard to be sure. They're sending him home as it's nearly over now anyway and he will need to recover."

"Home." Maura had to fight to stay upright in the chair. She was exhausted. Distraught. Cameron was gone; he'd left his daughter. And … and Abraham was coming home. "When?"

"You should lie down a while. Let me fix you something to eat to refresh yourself before anything further is said or done."

"No, it's … it's my house. I … the coffee should be ready." She didn't smell it, though, and looked over. She'd forgotten to finish it.

Mr. Luchner stood and helped her up, walking her out of the kitchen and to the parlor where the afghan lie on the floor in front of the chaise. He sat her down on it, picked the afghan up and helped to raise her feet as she leaned back against the pillows. Numb. Tired.

Cameron was gone. Her Cameron. The children … they would be Abe's now. How injured? Was he another who would need extra care? She couldn't bear to think of him that way and tried not to think. He was coming home.

To treat her like family.

And why not? His father treated her like a daughter. She let her eyes close. Only a few moments before Samantha would wake.

She woke to the baby's cry and bolted up.

Mr. Luchner held the child and stroked her head. "She rolled over and got a small bump. Nothing to be alarmed about. Rudy." He waited for the boy's attention. "Go and warm Miss Maura a cup of coffee, please."

Rudy planted a kiss on his sister's head and ran off.

The sun's placement told her she had closed her eyes more than a few minutes and she turned toward the grandfather clock. After eleven. "Oh." She ran fingers along her hair. It had to be a mess. "I am sorry. You should have woken me. Samantha must be starving by now."

"Not at all. She had her breakfast. Young Rudy is a wonderful help. He knew where to find everything and what she would want. Are you feeling better?"

"Oh." Maura felt dazed. She had no idea how to answer.

"You are not yourself yet. Allow me to bring you a tray along with your coffee." He set the baby on a blanket on the floor. "Miss Samantha, you behave now."

"Please, I should ask you if you need anything. I'm afraid I am being a terrible hostess." Maura pushed to her feet.

Mr. Luchner came to her. "I am not here for you to entertain."

"If you don't mind my asking, why are you here? And I don't mean to be rude…"

He gave her a grin and set a hand on her shoulder, something most men would never dream of doing. Even her father hardly ever touched her. "I am here because my Abraham asked me to look after you if you came to me. I expected you would not and told him so. He expected I was right. I left it as you wish, until I heard of the break in. If Muhammad will not go to the mountain…."

His face changed, grew serious. "There is no great love for the Terrys around this town. I am afraid that will reflect on his child, and now, on you. If his family were to stand with you, there would be no concern. However, with them against you and the town rather too narrow minded, you should not remain here on your own. Cameron did have some respect, enough they have left you alone. I believe Abraham's acquaintance with him was helpful in that case. Now though…"

"But I have been more than helpful at the home. I have cared for so many in town. Everyone has always been polite and friendly. I don't understand…"

"You and your father are new to the area. They respected his money and his position. Therefore, they would not have dreamed of bothering you."

"But everything belongs to me now."

"Until you marry and your husband takes control, or part control, and they believe, judging from your friendship with young Cameron, your choice may be…"

"Husband. I have no need of a husband. None of the men here

hold any interest for me, especially now that they have all turned their backs after I have done so much to help them all. I want none of them. If not for the children, I would have left long ago."

"Alone?"

"Alone. I am alone anyway, other than the children."

He tilted his head. "No. I have no interest in their petty opinions, either. Never had. Although they resent it, they respect me for it. If I take up as your guardian, they will not dare bother you, particularly those ungrateful Terry boys."

"But I cannot ask you..."

"You have asked nothing of me. My Abraham asked it. There is no one in the world whose opinion I respect more than my son's. If it has importance to him, it has the same importance to me. So." He stepped away. "Go and refresh yourself and when you return, we'll have something to eat. Then we'll get to work straightening the house."

Maura stood quietly a moment. He did it for Abraham. Then she wouldn't argue. She couldn't ask his father to go against his wishes if it meant so much to him.

It wasn't until she returned to the kitchen, bathed and changed, that she considered how much he meant to look after them. With a swallow of coffee, much stronger than she would have made it, she came to her senses. "I must ask, out of curiosity, how you intend to be our guardian living out in the country as you do."

He gave her a light nod. "I quite hope you will agree to come out to the farm to stay."

"The farm. But what of the house? If I leave it..."

"You could hire someone to look after it. They may, if you and the children are not here."

Leave the house. To go to Abraham's farm. With his father. She shook her head. "I'm sorry. I cannot. This..." She swept a hand to motion toward the room in specific and house in general. "This is all I have. I cannot leave it to someone else's care, or miscare. I must stay." If she could be honest, she had no interest in the house any longer. Going to the farm, though, would look as though she expected far too much from Abraham and his father. She would never presume. Whatever the town thought, she was a lady and would remain that.

Mr. Luchner frowned slightly. "You won't mind, then, if I stay here in the house with you?"

"Stay here?" Maura nearly dropped her coffee. He was

virtually a stranger.

"I am an old man, dear. You have nothing to worry about from me."

"Oh." She felt herself flush. "I didn't mean to imply…"

He grinned. "It was a joke. You'll have to learn not to take everything I say seriously." His chest rose and fell hard. "I may be an old man, but I am a skilled marksman still. The town knows I am. If they know I am here, you'll have no trouble. I noticed a room around the corner, on the main floor away from the rest…"

"Yes. My father stayed there when he could no longer use the stairs. It was a library and his bookwork room before that."

"Would you be upset to pass it along for the present time?"

"No. He has no further use for it. Neither do I."

"Then that will work fine."

"It's nothing fancy. There's barely anything in it."

"Then it shall be much like my own." He grinned and swallowed coffee.

Watching him, Maura considered whether she should protest the old man comment. He was not old. He did have a slight limp and she didn't dare ask what caused it. But his face was young enough, overly tanned from years of working in the sun, but firm yet. His hands didn't shake in the slightest. His shoulders were straight instead of slumped as many men his age and younger. He was still an able man, it seemed.

"If I can ask." She followed his movement into the kitchen. "What about your farm? Who will run it while you're away? Or do you plan to drive out during the day and back in the evening?"

"There is not much left on the farm to need tending. I can no longer plant and care for crops on my own so there have been none since Abraham left. I have not had but a small number of animals for years. I will ask the next farm to care for them for now and I'll leave a few in payment when I return. If I don't return, they'll be theirs to keep. We have talked of it already. It's a fair arrangement."

"But you cannot do that for my sake!"

"I do it for my son. He is away giving all he has for all of us. It would be little to do for him in return."

"Not all." Maura sat again. "He is coming home. You said he would."

The corners of his mouth twitched upward. "Yes. Not all. Thank the Lord, not all."

twenty

As he finished packing Cameron's belongings, Abraham sat on his friend's cot and dropped his head in his hands. His shoulder stung at the movement. It would remain a scar, they said. Not nearly as deep as the scar in his mind from how he received it. He'd refused to go home as they offered. It was nearly over. After what his friend did, Abraham owed it to stay till the end. He wasn't ready to go home. Home to Cameron's children. To the daughter who would never know her father. Abe had to wonder if Cam's family was even grieving. He had his doubts, although there had to be some kind of love there. There had to be. Cam was the oldest child. He'd done much to help the younger ones, given so much of himself. They had to at least have respect for that.

He shoved a hand through his hair and stood again, cradling his left arm so as not to let the stitches pull.

"Mail call."

Abe told the boy to enter and thanked him for the letter. One. From his father. Abe set it on the stand he'd made for Cam to match his own when his friend had insisted. What would he do with them? Leave them to rot in the sand? Might as well, he supposed. He couldn't carry them back. So far, he couldn't even carry his ruck. It was against doctor's orders. He would pull the stitches. A hell of a lot of stitches.

He'd been only semi-conscious while they stitched it. That was something to be thankful for, although it nearly amused Abe to be thankful for a blunt force hit to his head that almost knocked him out. The pain was bad even semi-conscious. They were low on morphine. He insisted the medic not give him any, although he was also surprised they listened since Abe wasn't sure how many medics he was talking to at the time. There'd been only one voice, but swirling faces hovered over him. Must have been one. The medic wouldn't answer about Cam, not until after Abe was done being stitched and had passed out and woken again.

Cameron. The reluctant soldier. He'd signed on only because Abe was going. His family tried to talk him out of it. Cam refused. He insisted on staying at Abe's side to watch over him, to "not let him have all the fun."

Abe sat again. Standing too long still made his eyes blur. Or the thought of how Cam gave his life for Abe's made his mind blur.

Leaning back against his pillow, he looked over at the letter. From his father. Not from Maura.

He sat up again, took it in his hands. She hadn't written in some time. Nothing came while he was recovering. During times he was coherent, he worried about her, about whether she had more trouble with anyone. She hadn't written.

Abe didn't bother to keep the envelope neat. He tore it open and unfolded it, then had to tell himself to breathe easier. The quickened pulse hurt his head. And his shoulder.

> *My Dear Son,*
>
> *I have been informed of Cameron's loss and send you my deepest sorrows as you mourn your friend and comrade. I also know of your injury and that you will recover, and for that, I thank the good Lord every day, and continue to pray for your safe return. You will forgive an old man, I hope, if I hold onto you too long upon seeing your face again. There has been much loss around here and much sorrow and no one will look askance at such a greeting. We all hold on to every bit of happiness we can find, even if it is not our own. I wish I could be at your side as you recover, both from your injury and from your loss.*
>
> *Moving on, as the thought of your return weighs heavy on my eyes and I will not be able to continue writing if I do not move on, I do want to let you know of a change in my situation.*
>
> *Miss Laerty, if you remember, had a scare some time back with strange men in town. Since, she has been much more careful and is never out alone. This appeared to help matters and she and the children were doing well.*

Abe's heart nearly stopped. *Were* doing well? *Were?* He grabbed a deep breath. It hurt his head.

> *Miss Laerty is not one to be held down easily. She is a nature seeker, as you are, as much in love with the old canyon as I have seen in you.*

Is. His father wrote of her in the present tense. He breathed a little more easily.

> *That being, she decided she must take the children out, in accompaniment of my friend Weathers and his daughter and*

grandson. They had a lovely day, I hear. While they were away, some fiend broke into the house and roughed it up. It seems nothing was taken, other than Miss Laerty's comfort being in her home, and something she will admit to no one else. I am certain she would want you to know. The intruder took only the stack of letters you and Cameron had sent to her. She had them saved in her room in the night stand and they are missing. She is rather concerned about why anyone would want the letters and who might want them. I have my feelings about the matter, which I will not say in print. As to why, I cannot be so certain.

I am aware of the gentleman you are and so have no fear about what they might find. She is quite upset, however. It seems she would rather they had taken everything else in the house but the letters.

Be that as it may, I cannot, in good consciousness, allow the young lady to still remain here alone with the children. I did offer her place at the farm, but although she now loathes the house to an extent, she will not leave it. I cannot say why on that count, either. She does seem to sleep knowing the Colt and I are on watch on the main floor.

I am unsure whether you will continue to write since your departure is imminent. That is, I do hope what I heard about your nearing arrival date is correct. If you do write, you will want to address it to me at the post office and I will gather my mail there.

It is with some sadness that I must tell you of the farm. There have been no crops this year other than my own small garden for vegetables, since the errant Terry lads decided I did not need their assistance. Also, since I am remaining in town with Miss Laerty as her guardian, I took the animals to be cared for at the neighbor's farm. They will hold them until my return, or until yours, with payment of a few to keep as their own, the number to depend on how long they feed and care for them. If you return and I do not, you are free to negotiate it as you wish.

I did want to leave things in better condition for you. Do not let this note worry you for my sake. I enjoy the children's activity and laughter, and Miss Laerty is a gracious hostess and charming. You might do well to stay involved with her after taking the children off her hands as is your obligation. They do love her so and it would be a shame to separate them after this time and what they have been through together.

Listen to an old man who doesn't remember his place. Let me continue with the thought I meant to write. I am not ready for the dirt yet, my son, in case the letter sounds that way. I am as well as when you left other than the longing in my heart to see you again. The children surrounding me daily does have me hoping for grandchildren of my own, as well. Of course as these will belong to you, I happily claim them and use that as my reasoning to stay here in town with Miss Laerty. A grandfather does have a right to protect his own. It is well understood and if criticized, I never hear of it.

Abe couldn't help but chuckle. No one would dare complain to his father about his actions. They weren't even likely to complain if he could not hear them.

Grandchildren. Yes, Abe supposed he was of the age for children of his own. However, having the two of Cameron's would be quite enough adjustment for some time.

There will be work to be done on the farm upon your return. I say your return, as I cannot leave Miss Laerty alone here even when the children go to the farm with you as they should. I will offer her space again. Perhaps your presence there would make it more comfortable for her to accept. Or perhaps less. I have put myself into a situation now that may be impossible to depart from until such time as she finds a young man who would be better company and support. She does seem to grow in fondness of my intrusion, however. We walk into town together and her chin is high as it should be and she will take my arm if someone – namely the young men in town – makes her nervous. It is good that my reputation has been well established already so there is no misunderstanding. Imagine. Because some men of my age who should know better by now have taken in young widows as their brides, too much speculation is passed around if a young widow dare speak to even an older gentleman. As I said, no one speaks such of Miss Laerty. Not since the one began that nonsense and I shut him down straight and hard.

You should not be alone with the children, either, and I try to work that around in my mind. I'm afraid I cannot and so shall have to leave it in your hands. I will not be offended if you decide you cannot care for the children and the farm on your own and so have to sell. I will be sorry life has thrown that circumstance at you – at us both – however, there are more important things than a piece of land we both love, that our ancestors have loved.

Well now, since I may have thoroughly plunged us both into a touch of dark, let me bring us out again before I close.

The children you have inherited are the most delightful I have had the pleasure of knowing since you were their ages. You are fortunate, indeed, to have such glowing life to return to. They will provide light in your path for many years to come, despite whatever misfortune comes along. Young Rudy is the most helpful boy and well-mannered. If you choose to stay on the farm, he will learn fast how to help you care for it. The girl is so young, an infant, so it may be possible to allow her to continue to stay with Miss Laerty in town to have constant care so you and Rudy are free to ... but listen to me again. As I said, it is your decision. I leave it fully in your hands and support whatever you decide.

This letter is much too long – a testament to how I look forward to seeing you. To holding you in my arms.

Take care, my son, and know whatever pain you have in your heart will mellow with time and with the love and care of these beautiful children. And of your father.

My Love to you,
Charles Luchner

Sell the farm? No. Abraham would never sell the farm. If he had to work to restore it every day of his life by himself, he would not sell it. That his father would even suggest such a thing said he had been alone too long, that he needed Abe's return more than Abe would ever have expected.

If he didn't return, Maura was there. And his father would choose to stay in town with her rather than let her stay in town alone. She must have some draw to make the man leave his farm, his whole world.

Someone ransacked the house to find letters he'd written her? Lying back on his pillow to ease the dizziness, Abe tried to imagine why anyone would want his letters. What had he said? Nothing personal, he didn't imagine. Although there was the one ... the one where he told her how her words were soothing, made him feel at home if only for a few minutes. He'd said how he enjoyed hearing from her. A light wave of nausea went through him. It could very well be taken as more than he meant it. But his last letter – the one she hadn't answered – spoke of being family to her. If they took them all, they would read that, as well. He had said nothing that could not be interpreted as fondness, as in a brother.

It came to Abe that he perhaps should not have mentioned the family idea. They could think as they wished. He had never cared before, and had no need to care now, particularly since they had all turned their backs not only on assisting Maura, but his father, as well. Abe had relied on the respect the town had for his father. He never would have thought he'd be so left alone as not to be able to keep the farm going.

He would be home soon. There was no use fretting about the whole thing now. Maura was safe with his father and his father's Colt watching over them. The rest, he would take care of when he was home.

Perhaps he should not have refused to return immediately.

twenty-one

Maura pulled a chair out at the table and handed Mr. Luchner a cool cloth to wipe the perspiration from his forehead. August's heat had filtered through to the first week of September and yet he insisted on walking to town with Rudy and Samantha. They needed the air, whatever it may be, he said. Maura believed he enjoyed showing them off as though his own grandchildren. She supposed they were now, by all rights. "Is there word from Abraham yet?"

"Nothing." The man sighed, concern blanketing his face. It had been over three weeks.

"He is still in mourning and may be unable to write, I suspect." With Samantha propped on one hip, she poured a glass of iced tea for each of them and sat across the table. "I know he is well. We would have heard otherwise. That is, you would have heard. The bad news always travels so fast."

"Yes. I am sure he is still well."

"And yet you are bothered by his silence."

"My own letter to him concerns me." His shoulders sagged only the tiniest bit. "I suggested he might want to sell the farm instead of caring for it alone with the children. He must be angry. Or hurt. It means so much to him."

"But why would you suggest selling? It means much to you, also. I know you miss it. You should go back instead of staying here for my sake."

He reached across the table for her hand. "Maura, dear, you have become like my own daughter. I would never leave you unprotected. Even if your windows have been replaced and your door repaired, neither will prevent the scoundrel from returning if he decides."

"You think he will?"

"Not as long as Colt and I are here. I am glad to see nothing has come of the letters that were stolen. Whoever took them must not have found what he wanted to find."

She shook her head and pulled a strand of hair from the baby's fist. "There was nothing to find. Other than ... his sketches. His beautiful words. There was nothing...." She rose to escape Mr. Luchner's eyes. As an excuse, Maura took cheese and bread from the cupboard and spread them on the cutting board.

"You need not hide your feelings from me." He had come up behind her.

A touch of her shoulder and she turned to him, unable to hide her emotions. His beautiful words were gone, irretrievable in all likelihood. And his sketches. Nothing anyone else would cherish. There was nothing to find. Too much of her had begun to wish there had been. And she wouldn't care if anyone knew. They all detested her now, as it was. What difference would it make? She'd done nothing she shouldn't have. She had not promised herself to Cameron. She had never deigned even the slightest kiss. Not from Cameron. Not from any man. Twenty-four years old, and she had never tasted even the chastest kiss.

Charles Luchner raised her chin with gentle fingers. "My son should consider himself the most fortunate man in town. I do hope he will realize he is, once he is past his mourning."

She wrapped around him, unable to control herself.

He tapped her back. "Dear Maura, please do yourself the favor of remembering Abraham has been away for some time, that he has been in war. That very often hardens a man beyond ... sometimes beyond what a woman can fully repair when he is again home. Be patient. He will be guarded with you as I taught him to be and more, as life has now taught him to be. Rest assured, as you wait for him to notice your feelings, that he is still inside. If you can bring him out again, it would do my heart good." He stepped back to see her face. "And rest assured, however hard he has become, he would always be good to you. I have no doubt he would be, if he has sense enough to allow you to give him the chance."

"Then you do not disapprove? We have not even met. I have seen him from afar while he was in town, admired him." She felt her face redden. "And I mean, I have admired the way he holds himself, the gentleness I have seen, the beauty of his creations, his carvings. But we have not met and I am acting like a silly schoolgirl. I'm afraid I'm embarrassing myself beyond repair."

He grinned. "Not at all. I have lived far too long for you to be embarrassed in front of me. I have seen far too much and understand more than perhaps I should. And if it will not embarrass your further, I feel the strong plea Abe sent me to watch over you was more than concern for a woman looking after his friend's child. It seemed much more. Although it could be only an old man's hopefulness."

Maura shook her head. She wouldn't allow herself to believe he thought more of her than as a relative. He had said so. "You are not an old man. You are still so very young. And Abraham will have his pick of girls when he returns. There are so many of us, and so few very eligible men. I am sure he will not have to worry about being at the farm alone. Any girl in town would be glad to have him and look after the children. I know they would. Many await his return. I have heard the talk."

"Have you?" He tilted his head as he studied her face. "I hoped you had not. I think, since you have heard, I might as well mention that the talk is much of the reason you are being ostracized. It is little to do with the children or Miss Sadie or young Cameron. It is because they fear Abraham could be drawn to you instead of to one of their unworthy daughters. And they are unworthy, dear Maura. None of those spoiled little girls with no thoughts of their own would be worthwhile enough for Abraham. He is intelligent enough to know. Why do you think he refused all advances before he left?"

"He refused because he didn't want to leave a girl in a compromised position. Cameron wrote to me such. If not for that, I believe he would have, in fact, cared quite a bit for Sadie. I believe he may grieve her still, as well, although he could never say so." She stopped. Moved away. "I am sorry. I should not have said it."

"Maura." Mr. Luchner moved up to her again. "If a man is going to care quite a bit for a young lady, he will do so no matter how often he tells himself he would not, or will not. If Abraham had been interested enough in Miss Monroe, she'd have known."

Maura lowered her head. "In that case, if he had any interest in me, I should know so, as well." Tired of the conversation, she picked up the cheese and bread board and took it over to the table barely in time for Rudy to burst in with his friend. "Go and wash and come sit. I need to put Samantha down for her nap."

+_+_+

"Luchner!"

Abe turned sharply toward his lieutenant. "Yes, sir."

"Pack it up. You're going home."

He stared. "Sir. But…"

"Why is it you did not tell me of your father's condition?" He moved steadily closer, striding across the sand.

"Sir?" Abe's heart pounded. It made his shoulder throb.

"He is alone, I hear."

"No, sir. Has something happened?"

"No? Your mother passed some years ago. Is that not right? And you have no siblings?"

"She did, sir. And I had two siblings. Both died of Scarlett Fever when they were young, before I was born."

"So you are an only child, responsible for looking after the welfare of not only your father but two young children?"

"Yes, sir. Corporal Terry's children. He willed them to me."

"They are in your elderly father's care, I just now hear. Your father who has been forced from his home for lack of being able to care for it."

"No, sir." Abraham started to argue, but it was nearly true. "Yes, he is ... he is in town now, looking after the children and the young woman Cameron named to care for them. They are all well."

"Are they?" His lieutenant looked as though he wanted Abraham to agree they needed him home. They didn't. They were doing fine without him, in town, the Colt at his father's side.

"Walk with me, Sergeant."

With a light nod, Abe stayed a half step behind but kept pace. They stopped out away from where other ears would pass close enough to hear.

"Now, drop the 'sir' bit and the guarded speech and talk to me, man to man."

Abe cast a frown. "I'm not sure I understand."

"Your shoulder is not healing as well as it should. I've checked with the medics."

"It was a deep wound. It will heal in time."

"Abraham, you do realize we do not need to have you here any longer. This is all wrap up and shut down. You have done your job well, valiantly. You deserve to go on home to your father and those children. I heard of the break in. It is a safety issue. Enough reason to send you home. There are enough children unprotected…"

"They are protected. My father is the best marksman in town, other than when I am home. They are well protected."

"I'll pretend I didn't hear that. Take this as an order, if you wish, but you are leaving. Today. Get packed and do not counter anything I say as I take you to the general to explain why you need to leave. Are we understood?"

"But there are men whose families need them more…"

"None have been here as long as you. None have given as much as you. I want you to go home now. If it's the only thing I can do for you, allow me to do that. If for no other reason, my conscience will be a touch more clean."

"There is no reason for your conscience to be anything other than clean."

"Corporal Terry followed my orders."

Abe stared. "Sir?"

"We could not fire without being fired on. I had him draw their fire. He was, of course, supposed to stay down lower, get down faster."

"He did."

"Not fast enough. I expected, of all the men, he could."

"He did." Abraham dropped his head and raised it. "I went after him."

"You what?"

"I was afraid he'd get his head blown off, so I went after him. To stop him. It was too late. They had seen him already and began to fire. We held our own out there for some time. He ... he learned well how to watch all around him, better than I expected. Until one of them closed in from behind. We didn't hear him. I didn't hear him. Cam did. He managed to keep the bullet from going into my heart where it was aimed." Abe swallowed and gritted his teeth. Then he grabbed a deep breath. "Your conscience should be clear enough. It is mine that is not, and it is why I cannot leave. He stepped in front of the bullet for me. Told me I damn well better live and go home to take care of his daughter. While he was bleeding to death in my place, his last words were about his daughter. I took him away from her. How do I go back to her now?"

His lieutenant stared, set a hand on his good shoulder. "You go back to her as the hero you are."

Abe started to argue.

"Luchner." The voice softened. "If Cameron had not saved you at that time in that place, you would not have saved those two dozen men and this battle would have been lost. We could not afford to lose this battle. You know as well as I do. It would have dragged this thing on much longer, with more lives lost."

"Cameron could have..."

"No. Abraham, Corporal Terry became a decent soldier with your help. He only lived as long as he did with your help and you risked your neck plenty keeping so close an eye on him. He would not have known how to handle the situation the way you did. None of us would have thought to do such a thing. I still wonder how you did."

"Elementary farm work. Hard to explain."

His lieutenant grinned. "No need. But we needed you. It's a damn good thing you were still alive to be there. You go home and tell his daughter that, when she's old enough, and you tell her how her father gave his life for you, how he wanted you to go home and take care of her. She will respect how much he respected you. She'll honor the memory of his bravery and his sacrifice, as she should. You go home to her. And to your father. Go take back your farm before it falls into the wrong hands."

"What?"

The lieutenant frowned. "You didn't know?"

"Know what?"

"There is a petition to release your farm to the town for auction since it is abandoned."

"No. They can't. It belongs to my father. It belongs to me."

"Go back and claim it. I have sent a letter ahead, urgent telegraph, saying you are on your way home to claim your property. You must go back now, Abe. You do not deserve any more loss resulting from all you have given. Go home."

Abe nodded. He wasn't ready to go home. But he would not let them take his farm away. He would not.

twenty-two

"Mr. Luchner!" Maura propped the baby against her hip and hurried up the stairs, into the front door, and to the parlor. He wasn't there. "Rudy, go out to the back and see if he's in the garden."

"Yes 'm." The boy hurried off.

Maura checked the bedroom. The door was open. It was empty. He had to be in the garden. Rudy would bring him. She set the baby in the playpen and talked to her to calm the child. Samantha hated being trapped. She was too much like her parents, always wanting to be in the middle of some adventure, usually something that would end in a bumped head. Maura didn't have time to comfort a bumped head right now. She needed to find Abraham's father.

Rudy ran back in. "He's not in the garden."

"No? Then where on earth would he be?"

"The car's gone."

The car. Maura began out toward the garage. "Stay with your sister." Where would he have gone without telling her? She said they wouldn't be long. She had some work to do at the home, a new baby to help care for, a young mother scared about how she would take care of it if the father didn't come home. Maura had sat with her for the longest time to show her how to care for the newborn and to encourage her that she was strong, she could take care of her child alone if needed, as Maura had, as many had. She would be there to help, at least for a while.

Maura looked into the garage. It was empty. Where had he gone? The telegram was still in her hand. It was from Abraham's unit, not from him. Her heart beat so fast she felt feint. She nearly tore it open, but it was addressed to his father. She couldn't. She hoped he wouldn't have a heart attack at the sight of a telegram from Abe's unit. She also hoped she wouldn't.

Pacing along the front porch, she considered whether it would be easier coming from her, if it was good enough reason to open it. But maybe it wasn't what she thought. Many telegrams had come. They were not all bad news. Usually, the town council knew before the family did. The council had heard nothing. At least they had said nothing.

The sound of a pattering motor that was nearly at its end caught her attention before she saw the car. Her heart pounded faster.

It made her head start to hurt. It sent nausea through her body. How could she give it to him? What if it was bad news?

Mr. Luchner didn't bother to pull the car into the garage. He stopped in the drive, turned off the engine and stepped out. "What is it, dear? Did I worry you? I didn't intend to be gone so long, not long enough for you to know I was."

Maura shook her head. It was all she could do.

"I have something for you." He gave her a grin.

She nearly cried as she watched him approach with something bunched in his hand. She couldn't look. She felt dizzy, hiding the telegram behind her back, near her side.

"Are you all right?" Mr. Luchner – Abraham's father – stood before her, watched her closely.

"I just came from town."

"Ah, has someone bothered you again? Tell me who it is and..."

"No."

"Then what is it, dear one? Can I show you first what I have that might make you feel better?"

She nodded. What else could she do?

He held up a bundle of letters. "I went to retrieve what belongs to you."

"Abraham's?"

"Yes. They promised me they were all there. It was a Terry boy, like I suspected. Turns out a girl he has interest in had her hopes on Abe. He wished to prove there was little reason for the girl to wait for him when Abe had his mind set on you. He didn't find what he wanted and nearly threw them out. His youngest brother rescued them."

Maura took the letters into her free hand and burst into tears. There. On the front porch, where anyone could see, she pulled the letters into her chest and rocked herself as well as she could on her feet. It was perhaps the only thing she had left of him.

"Come inside, dear." Mr. Luchner half pushed her in through the door and settled her on the chaise. He called for Rudy to bring iced tea. "I should not have told you. Or did I worry you? I cannot imagine you would worry so over an old man."

She sniffed and set the letters in her lap to wipe at her nose. With shaky fingers, she handed him the telegram. "This came today. It's not from Abraham. It's from ..."

"His unit." His hands trembled as he took it and studied the outside.

"It cannot be … they would know by now. They always know first, before the telegraph comes. They always know. They didn't…" She wiped at her nose.

With a deep rise and fall of his chest and shoulders, Charles Luchner tore the envelope open. "We may as well find out."

Maura continued to rock herself, eyes closed, tissue pressed to her face.

"He's coming home."

Her eyes snapped up. "What?"

"This is a cease and desist note about the farm, Abraham's claim on it. He's on the way."

Maura could no longer control herself. The tears took over, became sobs. She leaned unabashedly on his father's shoulder; his arm wrapped around her. He was coming home. He was on the way. Of course he very well had no interest whatsoever in her, other than as caregiver for the children, but it no longer mattered. It did. But it would be all right as long as he was home. As long as he was safe.

She was barely able to clean herself up enough to accept the iced tea. She heard his father tell Rudy what was happening so as he wouldn't worry. Rudy jumped up and down, the baby in his arms. Samantha laughed. It was the first time Maura had heard her laugh, although Rudy said she did.

Abraham was coming home.

"There is something else."

Maura studied Mr. Luchner's eyes, trying to decide if it was a good something or a bad something. She couldn't quite tell.

He pulled a single letter from his jacket pocket. Unopened. It was Abraham's writing, addressed to her. "It was grabbed from the mail before it could be delivered. He nearly opened it, but the youngest stopped him."

Maura saw her hand shake as she took it. She was being ridiculous. A silly school girl.

Mr. Luchner stood. "Come Rudy; let's take Samantha out to the garden for fresh air." He gave Maura a wink.

She sat and stared at the writing. The date. It was sent only two days after the last she'd received. Why had he written again so soon? Her hands continued to tremble as she opened it, not carefully enough. It tore along the back. She didn't care if it did. Why had he written again so soon? She pulled it from the envelope, placed it to her nose and closed her eyes while she took in its scent.

Finally, she brushed moisture away from her lids and unfolded it.

My Dear Maura,

Please forgive me for writing you again so soon, but I am alone now without Cam here as company and am on limited duty while my shoulder heals, so I am at loose ends with my time. I am fortunate the injury was to my left shoulder so as to be able to write legibly. It will heal. The medics are uncertain it will heal well and think it may cause trouble for years to come. I tell them it will not. I have always healed well, and quickly, and see no reason not to do so again. Why do I tell you this? Because I believe you have dealt with enough injury to not wish to worry about mine as well.

Again, I beg your patience. I am aware, once I am home – if that happens as they say it will – you may very well have had your fill of my rambling and presence of sort. I shall understand and shall respect your wishes. Please know I understand the bond you have with the children who are now legally in my care and I do not wish to keep you from them. I have few qualms as far as taking young Rudy onto the farm and under my wing. The baby, I do have to admit frightens me at the thought. I am but a young single man with no experience with children, especially of such young children who do not, as yet, understand the English language. I do wonder if it would be a burden on you to continue to ask for your help for some time until I believe the infant will be safe enough under my care.

Of course I do not mean I would cause her actual harm. Heaven forbid. I only mean as far as being so unsure what to do with an infant. This causes me no little amount of worry, I will admit. However, with your guidance, if you allow, I will learn what I must for immediate purposes and try my best to work up to the rest. We shall grow together, Samantha and I, and shall figure it out if I can get past the big hurdle.

There is another reason I write so soon after my previous letter. I believe it may be far too pertinent, even for me, however, and I am stalling while I consider whether to approach the subject.

My father – and here is another stall – has considered selling the farm. I did write him a brief note requesting he do nothing until my return. Of course, if I do not return, then I will have no say. However, I am unsure how attached you are to staying in town and I understand if so. If not, and if Father insists on selling, I would like to make you a one of a kind offer. An exchange, if you will. Buy it from him for one dollar and do as you can to keep it for Rudy and Samantha. It should rent well enough to pay for its needs. There is no mortgage on it. Upkeep will be the biggest expense. If you know of a young family in need of a nice place who will care for it in return for living there until Rudy is old enough to take it on, that may be your best option.

It is a lot to ask and I have no right. However, I trust no one else. You may wonder why I entrust you when we have not yet met. Simple matter. Your care of Cameron's feelings when he tried to persuade you to accept more from him than you wished, added to your care for the child resulting from a rather unfortunate night, as well as your constant care of those at the home ... all of these tell me more than I need to know. You have care of the children. Nothing is more valuable than that, particularly not a piece of land.

I have not written all of this to my father, as I am not sure he has any seriousness in the thought of selling. He lacks company. Or he did until coming to your rescue which I believe was more his own than yours. He loves the land as I do. Please keep that in your thoughts if he talks of it to you.

I should come to my main point, but I think I cannot as of yet. Instead, I will tell you of a rather large package I hope to have shipped home. I am unsure whether I'll be able to do so. If it works and if I do not follow it home, I want it to be yours to keep or sell as you wish.

They are a pair of night stands. Why would I ship night stands all the way overseas? I am somewhat embarrassed to admit why. They were hand carved. I had only meant to do the one that sat beside my cot. Carving on its sides filled empty hours. They are not good carvings. Most of those hours were by firelight in shadow. I would not consider bothering with it, except Cameron begged me to make one for him to match. After some denying I had any interest, I of course gave in to him. They are a matching set. Not the same, but similar enough. You see, they depict our lives, our different yet same lives. I believe when you see them together, you will know which is his and which mine. It is not vanity that makes me determined to try to send them back, but Cameron's memory. He made such a fuss over them. More than they deserve.

The remark I wrote in the last letter was, I feel, undeserved and untrue. I have never had relative feelings toward you. That is, feelings of you as a relative.

There. Now I've said it and will move on. Perhaps you're skimming this monstrosity of rambling thoughts and will not even see it. That may be just as well. I have been here far too long and ...

And dear Maura, nothing makes me want to return home now nearly as much as the thought of finally meeting you in person. I will hope you will not turn the other way and ask me not to interfere in your life more than I have already.

I should not send this. It grows late and I am weary and sick-hearted and exhausted from being a leader of men with my strong, proud front when inside I wish to run from here as fast as I can go and return to the farm, the canyon, out away ... away from gunfire and hard cots and blowing sand and the cold chill I feel returning and men bleeding and crying out for their loved ones.

Apologies again. I am quite sure you do not wish to hear of it more than I wish to continue seeing it. You have seen enough yourself, I am sure, and I applaud your work as you help those who have returned in need of care. I assure you, if I go home, I will be fully able to care for myself, or I shall not return to you. To town. It may be pride, which may be sinful, but I will not...

I am thinking too much now of home. It is not helpful to my current situation where I am in flux as to where I will be in a few days. My father warned me, before I left, to protect my heart above all else. I have done my best but fear I am now failing that task. I fear the thought of your face within reach of my own is disturbing my judgment. My heart is interfering with my duty. It tells me to take my lieutenant's offer to claim my shoulder and head are too injured to work properly and safely. However, neither is true.

Neither is true. I am more careful than need be with my shoulder for the purpose of allowing it to heal well enough it will not be a long-term problem. The farm awaits.

And again, I am rambling. Stalling. Not wanting to end this letter and therefore my only very small connection with you, someone who is very well an enigma I rest my thoughts upon in too much haste. I do not keep hopes of anything in reality. It is only in my nightly thoughts, as I lie here alone in this tent – I refused a new tent mate unless it becomes a necessity – that I allow myself to step out of where I am, of who I am. For I am aware I have nothing to offer you.

I will stop there. I must stop there. If I am of my right mind in the morning, I shall burn this instead of sending it. If you have read thus far, be kind enough to realize I am nursing a concussion that has impaired my judgment and if we are to run into each other, I would consider it a favor if you were to forget everything I have just said.

I shall burn this in the morning. Tonight, I am too tired to move from the cot.

And so I close and will set it on my night stand where the envelope awaits it addressed and stamped. In the morning, I shall seal it tight and toss it on the fire.

So good night, sweet Maura. If this has served no purpose but to help me think of you in my dreams and assist my sleep, it will have been worth every bit of wasted ink and paper.

With my kindest regards,

Yours,

Abraham

Maura sat and stared at his name. At *Yours, Abraham* – yours. It was not … not a brotherly letter. It was as if from a lover, as well as she could imagine. She had never had a letter from a lover, but … this was as if from a lover.

Her eyes watered, overflowed. *Her face within reach of his own.* Yes. She wanted her face within reach of his. She wanted to open his shirt and check his shoulder herself, to see how bad the injury was and if she could help it along. To touch his skin.

Her face warmed, burned. She brought the letter up to her nose to hide, to smell him.

He did not have brotherly feelings toward her.

"*Yours, Abraham.*" She studied it again.

Hers.

Perhaps he would be.

And perhaps, as he said, it was only the concussion, the homesickness. The longing to connect with another soul in a way she hadn't yet. Perhaps he was only feeling the same. Lonely. It didn't mean, once he got home, he would have real interest. He made it clear he may not, although he set it on her lap as though she might not.

Perhaps she wouldn't. When they were face to face, perhaps there would be nothing there to act upon, or to wish to act upon. Words on paper did not say as much as those spoken face to face. They were too easy to act as though they weren't real, that they were imagination and generalizations and longings looking for a home. She would not believe otherwise.

His father warned her. Be patient. He will have hardened. Abraham didn't sound at all hardened. He sounded … gentle and strong and willing to care for and be cared for and … and beautiful.

She looked at the letter's date again. Nearly six weeks ago. And she hadn't written him back. She didn't know he had sent this. It was nearly lost. He hadn't burned it as he said he would. Maura wondered why he decided not to do so. And she wondered if he was hurt that she did not write back.

He wouldn't come home if he couldn't care for himself? Maura cringed. She should have received it so much earlier. She should have written and demanded he come home however he could. She would gladly care for him.

twenty-three

Maura stroked the new baby's head as she washed him. A large infant, this one was. Good thing his mother was not a dainty woman. She was also not a frightened girl as most Maura had cared for. It was her third child, conceived purposely before her husband left for the war. She'd said she knew it would be a boy and named the child after the husband. The husband was on his way home, as Abraham was supposed to be. The timing suited the woman fine. She would have time to recover enough to be well on her feet to greet him and set his son in his arms.

They had heard nothing from Abraham since the telegram announced he would be home soon. It had been long enough, she thought. They should at least have word.

Pushing it from her mind as well as she could, Maura wrapped the clean infant and took him squalling to his mother. She couldn't help but smile at the scene. It was nice to see such a normal birth for a change, a confident mom and healthy baby with a father still live and standing on his own. Part of her wished to see them greet each other. Most of her did not. Unless she had word from Abraham first.

"Maura, dear, you must sit and rest a while. You've been on your feet all day."

She grinned at Miss Jeanne, the only supervisor still at the home since the "restructuring" Maura had heard of but tried to keep distance from. The atmosphere was so much more pleasant since and Maura spent more time there again. Part of it was Samantha's age. At five months, she did well with Rudy and Mr. Luchner watching her. At times, she visited with the Weathers or came along with Maura so the boys could go off and take care of some project they were doing together. They wouldn't tell Maura what it was.

She also worked so many hours now because of Abraham's letter, because he had praised her for the work. It made her feel guilty when she read it since she had been away too often. Being back, keeping her hands busy and constructive, helped her get through the days, helped her think she was assisting Abraham in some small way, that she was pulling herself back up far enough in the town's eyes to not be a horrible match for him.

If anything he said in the letter was real and not concussion-induced prattle. And she still believed it was entirely possible she would feel no more than admiration for him upon their meeting.

If they met.

At times, like now when there had been no word and it had been so long and all of his mentions of feeling he would not come home again sank in, Maura believed he would not. Much of her believed he would not. Part of her had considered how she should be more open toward other young men in town, those still able to stand on their own, the smart, gentle, strong, caring ones. Not that she saw many she believed could possibly fit that description well enough. And maybe Abraham wouldn't, either. Maybe much of what he was in her mind was only in her mind, a dream she had hoped for and found too easily in words.

With a sigh, she gave into Miss Jeanne's badgering to sit and rest. Only for a few minutes. There was too much work to be done.

+_+_+

Abraham thanked the porter for helping him lug the heavy objects off the train onto the platform and for calling to someone who would assist him the rest of the way. The man had a motorized coach, he said, and could pack him and his luggage wherever he needed to go. With Abe's thanks, the porter gave him a bow.

"No sir. Thank you for doing what you've done for all of us. And for returning again whole. Ted will give you a nice discount for your trip, as well. His boy is still there, you see. Having any of you come back who look this good encourages him.

Abe grinned. "It is near the end. If his son still stands now, he should be home soon, in good shape, as well."

The porter nodded toward Abe's wrapped shoulder. "It'll be all right again, I hope."

"It's nearly all right now. Not taking chances with it."

"Good for you. Be well. And welcome home, son." He tapped him on the good arm. "Ted, got a soldier needs a ride. Can you help him out?"

A man with silver hair turned and grinned; his shoulders straightened. "Sure thing." He took Abe's hand in thanks and praise, asked what he had to transport, eyed the night stands wrapped up in heavy paper and yelled over to a couple of boys playing ball in the grass beside the station.

With the man's insistence Abe not lug any of the baggage, he and the boys got it loaded and helped him up to the seat. The boys jumped onto the back to support the luggage they'd tied in well. And they were underway. Abe felt his stomach lurch at the thought.

He was going home.

He did his best to talk with the man and boys, to relate experiences without graphic detail, to talk about plans and outcomes and strategy. He didn't want to talk about it. He was nearly home, his mountains in view around him, the canyon not far away. He wanted silence, to revel in the nature, the tumbleweeds, the scattered trees, the bits of greenery along ridges in the rocks. The fresh air. He breathed it deeply into his lungs and held it as the wind brushed along his face. It smelled of the mountains from a distance. Soon, he would go up in them.

When he talked about doing so back in camp, the others thought he had finally lost his mind for wanting any more to do with a tent and cot and sleeping in the dirt. No cot, Abe told them. Only they hard ground beneath his sleeping bag, with a small fire outside the tent to keep critters away, and to heat coffee in the morning. Or if it was nice, he would sleep outside the tent next to the fire and watch the glowing white stars pierce the black of the night sky. In camp, there was always too much haze in the sky to see much of anything. The stars, when visible at all, were blurred, indistinct. Abe looked forward to sitting outside as it grew dark and simply staring up at the sky from home.

Home.

They were growing near. He had meant to send a telegram to his father along the way, once he was inside the States again. Somehow, he couldn't allow himself to do so. He wasn't home yet until he reached the farm. He wouldn't count however many chickens he had left until he got there.

They were close enough it would be a short distance to the canyon and he considered asking the driver to take him over just long enough to look at it. But that would wait. He would – if she agreed – take Maura and the children the next day for a picnic, one like those she'd written of. The thought of it made him clench his eyes.

"Are you all right, son?"

He opened them and nodded at the driver. "Yes."

"It's been a long time, has it?"

"Sixteen months."

"Place has changed. At least town has changed. I come in now and then. Nice little diner here now the wife likes for something different. Wasn't there when you left. Give it a try. Tell them I sent you and they'll treat you extra nice."

Abe grinned. He didn't answer. What he wanted was a home cooked meal, even if he had to do it himself as he often did after he and his father had been out working. They each had their specialties, but his father's specialty list was quite short and Abe grew weary of it if he let his father cook too often. He knew it was a ploy: a good way to get Abe to volunteer to cook. Of course, having someone else cook who knew better how to do it would be all right with him, too.

He pushed that thought aside as the driver headed the direction of town. "No, go left here."

"Left?"

"To the farm. I want to see that first."

"Not much out that way anymore. An abandoned place."

"It only looks abandoned. It isn't. It's mine. My father's legally but mine now. I am taking charge of the place. He has earned his rest and to ramble around on it only as he wishes."

The man stared at him a moment, then gave him a light nod. "He'll be glad to see you again, I'm sure."

"Yes, and me him."

"Any missus in your life?"

Abe grabbed a deep breath. "Perhaps." He wouldn't say more, and the man didn't ask, although the boys behind him chuckled.

As the farm came into view, Abe's shoulders – weary as they were – straightened. His farm. Home. He could barely keep himself from jumping out and running down the old dirt path he'd walked part way out of until Cam stopped to pick him up. It seemed ages ago. Running would make him more weary, though. And there was much to do this day before he could lie down and rest. It was early still. He had traveled all night, sleeping off and on. There was time to get things done before nightfall.

The wagon rattled up close to the porch and came to a stop.

Abe sat and stared at the place. Run down. Yes. His heart jumped between elation and melancholy at its state. He could never ask a lady to come to the farm as it was. It would take weeks of fixing up to be ready for guests.

"Sure this is the place?"

He glanced over at the man. "Yes. It didn't look like this when I left. My father is so meticulous. But he's been staying in town."

"Some elbow grease and it'll be good as new. Want any of this stuff left here or do they continue into town?"

"All of it stays. As do I." He got down off the wagon.

"Stay? And what will you do out here alone? No horses, it looks like. No car unless it's back in one of those sheds."

"I'll manage." He tried to take one of his bags from the back.

The man hollered at the boys to get them, again refusing to let Abe carry anything. And he insisted on walking into the house with him, to check for intruders, he said, his shotgun on his arm.

There were no intruders. Everything was nearly as he left it. There wasn't even a heavy coat of dust as he'd expected. There was no dust. It had been recently cleaned. No spider webs. He walked to the kitchen and opened the pantry. Cans were there. Clean and new.

"Someone's taken care of the place inside anyway."

Abe nodded. "Thank you for the ride and the help. What do I owe you?"

The man motioned toward the boys carrying in the night stands. "Tell them where they go. I don't want you to move stuff around until that shoulder heals. Will you have help? You cannot fix this up yourself."

"I can move them all right, thank you. You've done enough already."

"Nonsense. They're strapping lads and love to prove their strength. Point out where they should go and they'll get them there."

Abe wanted one to go to Maura, the other to his father, but he didn't want to have to explain that much. They could go in his room for the moment. He led them there and stopped at the door. His father's belongings were in his room. With a frown he walked around running his fingers along the furniture that had been moved. Not by his father. Surely, he wouldn't have taxed himself so. "Set them down a moment." He went past the boys and walked to the opposite end of the house to find his father's room. Abe's things were there. His furniture. His sketches that had been tacked against one wall. They now adorned one wall lined with cork board. The large bed was still there, though, with the single remaining in his.

His father's way of handing over control? Switching rooms was unnecessary. And he couldn't allow his father to downgrade himself in his own house, the house his father had owned. The house he'd been born in. They both had been, he and his father, both born in the third bedroom that was an office and guest room, not that they had guests much and there was the small guest house a few paces away from the main house. It likely was full of dust, however, as it normally was.

"Do you want them in here instead?"

Abe turned to the taller boy's voice. And he stared. He wasn't sure what to do with them, where to put them. "No. Leave them in the other room. Wait." He stopped the boy. "Bring them in here." Abe followed and pointed out the guest room. For now. Until he figured things out.

Returning the main room, he saw the man walk back in.

"Guess I was wrong. You do got a car in the shed. Filled with gas even. Looks used recently and ready to go."

Abe grinned. He wondered how long his father had been prepared for his arrival. The telegram apparently came through fine. "Thank you. What do I owe you?"

"Not a thing."

"Oh, no, I wouldn't dream of…"

"I know who you are. Wasn't sure until we got close to this place. Sergeant Abraham Luchner. The one who saved a ton of boys during that last big battle. My son was one of them. There are lots of us waiting to thank you for saving our boys. This is the least I can do. Anything else you need, you give me a holler." The man handed him a card with name and address. The last name looked familiar.

"It's not necessary. I was doing my job like everyone else."

The man hugged him tight. "You take care of yourself now. Find a nice young lady and have a good family and be happy." He backed up. "And don't hesitate if you need any little thing. Come on boys, let's leave the man alone and let him settle in."

Abe watched them go with a wave and turned back to his farm, his home. It was quiet. Too quiet. As much as he thought he'd want plenty of quiet with no explosions, no gun shots, no yelling, no crowds of men around him all trying to stay safe and watch over each other, Abe was too flooded by too much quiet.

He went back out of the house and surveyed the land. No crops. He sighed. There would be next season. And maybe he'd go ahead and put in some winter crops, just a few patches of broccoli and cauliflower, enough there would be something planted on the farm. Before he did anything else, he would go over and retrieve their animals, as many as still belonged to them. He would do that now, before he went to town to gather his father and the children. It needed to be home again first.

Closing the front door, he went to find the car and the keys that hung where they always had, and climbed inside. He hoped he remembered how to drive the thing. It argued before starting but he got it going all right. It needed work. Another thing to add to his list.

Jumping out onto the dirt road, he rolled the window all the way down in order to smell the fresh country air and took off toward the neighbors.

Not a bad deal, he supposed. They hadn't lost too many animals in exchange for care. Actually, he figured it was a heck of a good deal, as much as grain prices had risen. Abe hoped they would level again now that things were settled. Expensive grain, before they had their own crops to feed the animals, would make things harder. So much needed to be done. The guest house hadn't been touched. It needed some support and cleaning before it could be used again. Perhaps Maura would agree to move into the guest house, at least. That wouldn't be improper. But then, it wouldn't feel right to have her out there alone, not too far alone, only a few steps away, but still too alone.

And that wasn't in his plans. She was a lady and deserved to be treated as the lady of the house. He darn well would treat her that way, too.

If she would allow. That, Abraham was highly unsure about.

He was awfully glad they agreed to load the animals in the trailer within the next half hour and bring them along. It gave Abe time to walk the fences and be sure there were no holes where they could get out. He didn't imagine there should be since they hadn't been used and no one had been around. His father would have at least kept those in good repair before he shipped the animals off. He wouldn't risk losing them or having them wander off and get hurt by a coyote or otherwise.

He walked at a quick pace, his shepherd-terrier mix at his feet. The neighbors said he'd escaped back over to his own home often to look for Abe and his father, returning for food and a bit of attention.

The fence looked good. There was still some grain left in the bin and it was still fresh enough, so he started to shovel some into the feeding troughs to give his animals a good welcome home. Doing so, he decided he was rather hungry himself.

Back in the house, he washed up and went to the cupboard. But he closed it again. He didn't want to eat alone. He'd been doing that since he lost Cam. He'd refused to go sit with others in the mess tent, although they asked often enough. They thought it was uppity, he supposed. That wasn't farther from the truth. He grieved for Cam. Still. He wanted his friend there to join him for their homecoming. He could have taken the guest house if he didn't want to go back home, as Abe was sure he didn't. It was big enough for Cam and Rudy. The little girl should stay in the main house with Maura. They could have the big room. Abe would take the guest room. That was if Maura would come. He was depending on that fact a little too much, he supposed. She had turned his father down when he asked her. Why would he agree to Abe when they hadn't even met?

It felt like they had. Her words touched him more than he could admit. He wanted her there, at the farm, not in town with his father. He supposed that would be best for the moment. He and Rudy would fix the place up and give Abe time to court Maura properly as he should. Yes, that would be much better. She didn't need to come back to a run down farm with no real possibilities for any time very soon. But it would have. Abe would make it strong again. It would return to the respect it once had, and deserved.

At the sound of truck tires on the dirt road, he went out to guide it back to the fence. Yes, it would soon be home again. Full of life. Prospering. Comfortable. A place where a woman would be proud to live.

Very soon. He would work sun up to sun down to make it happen. And then he would invite her to come … to come live with him. Not only at the farm, but with him. If she would have him.

Satisfied the animals were settled in and safe by themselves, Abe told the dog to stay and watch after them, then went back to wash up again. This time he changed out of his clothes into something cleaner. He started to put on his old jeans that were still in his drawer, but looked over at his dress uniform and changed his mind. His father would appreciate seeing him in it. He had refused to leave town in uniform, at least until he was actually heading out, because he felt he hadn't earned the right yet. He supposed he had by this time.

He was no hero, as the man from the next town said, but he had done his best. He only wished Cam was still there so he could feel like he'd done better than his best. It would never quite be good enough without his friend returned with him.

Abraham grabbed a breath deep enough it made his lungs ache and released it. He shot a quick apology up to the sky, imagining his friend could hear, or hoping he could, and then pulled into his dress greens. Even through the foggy mirror that needed to be cleaned or replaced, he had to admit he made a sharp enough image. He would surely draw attention. Maybe he should go back to his own clothes.

They were his own clothes. He'd earned the right to wear them at his own homecoming.

And his father would be proud.

Swallowing hard, he headed back to the car, threw a glance over to the animals milling around munching on grain or lazing in the dirt. They were as content to be home as he was, he imagined.

The trip took longer than he felt it should and yet it was too fast. He was nervous. He was even more nervous than during any day he was overseas, even with gunshots buzzing past and rockets exploding and men dropping not far from him, he had never been quite so nervous. He had lost his mind. After all those many months he'd managed to keep his sanity, now he'd lost it. Maybe he wouldn't be good enough for Miss Laerty. She needed stability, not some man who shook in his boots at the thought of seeing her in person.

Still. She didn't need to be alone, either. And he could not take the children away from her. She would possibly accept him only to be able to remain close to the children.

He frowned as he took in the edge of town. He didn't want her to accept him for that reason. He'd have to be sure she knew right off that she could see the children whenever she wished, that maybe Samantha would be best in her care for some time yet, if she agreed.

But he had already told her that. In the letter. The letter that got mailed while he was still drowsing, when the clerk came in to ask if he had anything outgoing and he pointed toward it before awake enough to remember he meant to burn it.

Abe stopped the car. In the middle of the road. He stopped. The letter went through. The one he'd said way too much. How could he face her? Would she take him as he said, that it was only grief talking and … and it wasn't. She would know it wasn't. A man didn't talk that way if he didn't mean it. At least Abe didn't. She would know that much about him by now, after so many letters.

With another hard swallow and deep breath, he figured he didn't have much choice. The children were his charge now. He would have to face her. And he wanted to find his father, to allow him to wrap his arms around Abe the way he had mentioned he would. Embarrassed? No. Abe would not be embarrassed. He would be glad to not have broken his father's heart by not returning.

He had at least accomplished that much.

Putting the thing back in gear, he eased on forward into town. A few people turned to look. They recognized the car, he supposed. And he was in full uniform. Word would spread fast. He hoped to find his father before the gossip did.

He supposed the Laerty place would be the best place to start. She was perhaps at work and he could talk to his father first. That would work well. He hoped, as he pivoted the car that direction, it would work out that way. As the house appeared, Abe stopped again. No. There was something he had to do first.

Turning toward the middle of town, he parked up in front of the general store and ran in to pick up what he figured his father hadn't splurged on since Abe had been away. He never had. He never bought it for himself. It was time he had it.

As he talked enough to be friendly and to make queries as to where his father might be, getting the answer he already knew, Abe pulled away and was stopped by a young girl with an arm full of wildflowers.

"Flowers for your girl, mister?"

He grinned at the girl dressed not warm enough for the chill in the October air and pulled out far too much to cover the bunch of flowers he accepted. Her mouth gaped.

"I have no change for this much!"

"No change needed, little one. How about you do me a favor?"

"Yes sir! Are you a real soldier?"

"I am. Or I was. I'm home now to stay."

"I bet you're real brave."

"No, just willing." He gave her a wink. "Do you know where the children's home is?"

"Of course. Everyone knows that. I help there sometimes when they need. I play with the babies and keep them from crying. I make them laugh with funny faces." The girl demonstrated.

"I imagine they appreciate that a lot."

"Sometimes. Sometimes they say I'm in the way and I have to leave. But not if Miss Maura hears them they don't. She always lets me play with the babies."

"Ah, so you know Miss Laerty well then."

"Yes, sir. Everyone 'round knows Miss Maura."

He grinned. "Will you do something for me?"

She tilted her head. "Is it something good? She's one of the nice'uns no matter what some say and I will not do anything that's not nice to her."

"I would sincerely hope you wouldn't. I only want to know if she's there today, at the home, and how long she will be staying. Can you check for me? But don't tell anyone you're checking or that you saw me. Can you do that?"

"Sure, I can! Easy! Wait right here. I'll run and come right back." She dropped the rest of her flower bundle just inside the door of the store and yelled at the clerk she'd be back for them.

"Wait." Abe grabbed her arm to slow her. "I'll be over there." He nodded toward a store across the street. "Meet me there."

A big smile crossed her face. And she ran off.

Abe checked both ways and paced across the road.

When the girl returned, out of breath, he was done with his business and took her to the soda fountain to buy her an ice cream. "Will you be all right here if I go ahead now?"

She nodded through shoving ice cream in her mouth. "I bet you make her cry."

Abe raised his eyebrows. "I hope I don't."

"Yeah you want to. Girls like to cry for good things since they have to cry too much for bad things. My mama says it's true."

"Well then, she must be right." He rubbed her head and left the shop, pausing only a moment for someone who recognized him.

Abe drove up in front of the Laerty house and breathed easier knowing Maura and the baby were at the home instead. He saw a young head pop out the door and back in. Rudy, he supposed. As he neared the front steps, his father came out onto the porch.

"Abraham." He held the porch beam for support. "You came home. You surely did. And look at you all decked out like something to be proud of. Not that I wasn't always."

With a grin, Abe went up the stairs and grabbed hold of his father. He knew there were neighbors staring, barging in on the private moment. He couldn't have cared less if he was the king of the world and they caught him kneeling to his father. The man deserved it for all he had done.

"My son. Everything is right again now. I have you home."

"Not everything is right." Abe pulled back, unable to hide moisture at his eyes. "Cam didn't come back with me."

"I know, son. I am sorry. But he will always be here with you." His father tapped his chest. "And his little girl has been waiting for a father. She will be lucky to have you step in for him."

"How is she?"

"A beautiful healthy little girl. Pulls up onto everything so we have to watch her every movement. Big hazel eyes, like Cameron's. She's with Maura at the home today."

"I meant…" Abe paused, unsure he should admit just what he meant. "Miss Laerty. She has had a hard time of it. Her letters said she was well but I do think she was being strong, more than she should have had to be…"

"Yes. But she is, Abe. A magnificent woman, as your mother was. You should get along well enough to handle the children together."

"I plan to ask her to move to the farm. If you have no objections."

His father eyed him. "I have none. However, she is a lady and you need to consider…"

"I know she is. I would never compromise her status." He looked over at the boy who eyed him from around the door. "You must be Rudy." Abe went to take his hand in a firm shake, getting a fair amount of firmness in return. "I hear you have been an exemplary help to Miss Laerty and my father."

"I have tried to be, sir."

"Abe. Call me Abe. I know I am your guardian now but you have proven yourself worthy to talk man to man. And I have every hope you will be happy on the farm as you learn how to help me run it. I want you to know all there is to know about how to keep a farm running. Think you can do that?"

"Yes, sir." He ducked his head slightly at Abe's gaze. "Yes, Abe. I'll do anything I can. My sister will go too, won't she? I did promise to take care of her."

"That will be up to Miss Laerty."

"But … but you are Samantha's guardian also. Miss Maura said you were."

"Yes. However, a little girl needs a mother more than a father, don't you think?"

He frowned. "I think she might need both."

Abe smiled at him. "You may be right."

"Son, let's go inside. We'll have some lemonade and you can rest yourself. You must be weary after … after everything."

"No. I'm home now. And there's much to do."

"It'll wait a day or two."

"I'm afraid it won't. I want my first night back to be at home and I want you to come home, as well, as soon as you can. If that's the case, there is something I must do. Or at least I must try."

"What is it that won't wait a day?"

He grabbed a deep breath. "I need to go and meet Miss Laerty.

It is high time, I believe." Seeing a hint of a smile on his father's face, Abe turned back to the car. They followed, insisting on going along.

twenty-four

Maura sighed and wiped blood from the floor. The baby hadn't a chance. It was born far too early from a mother who had delivered not long enough before she became pregnant again. And she knew the girl wouldn't listen about abstaining for a few months so as not to take another risk.

With the floor clean, she scrubbed her hands and arms hard and shoved hair out of her face. The day had been too long already. She was too tired, but there was still much to be done and she didn't want to go face another night at home as mistress of a house with no master and no chance of one, unless she gave in to one of the offers from a returned soldier. A couple of them might do, she supposed, but she felt nothing but respect for them. At least she felt that. With some, she couldn't feel that much. She could hardly feel anymore. Except for her Samantha, who wasn't hers.

She grabbed a deep breath and dried her hands, wishing for a shower and fresh clothes and a hair brush. She was a horrible mess, not that it mattered. Those she cared for weren't concerned about how she looked. They only wished to be taken care of, which made her entirely too weary. But then, what else would she do?

"Miss Laerty?"

She looked up at her supervisor. "Yes?"

"There is someone here who wishes to speak to you a moment."

"Oh, Miss Jeanne, please assign someone else. I have had my fill for today. For the next two years, if truth be told. I need to go home and..."

"I'm afraid this one will accept no one but you. I must insist." The older lady came over and took her arm. "Would you like to make yourself presentable first?" She glanced at Maura's hair falling out of the bun.

"I have no energy to be presentable."

"But dear, you might..."

"Anyone who demands my personal attention shall simply have to take me as I am. I have been bedraggled for months. There is no further need to try to pretend otherwise." Maura dropped the towel over the sink and headed out to the main room, yanking the sheet that separated their private space out of her way.

She stopped at the sight of a man in uniform. A dress uniform. And a man on his feet, of no need for assistance ... a strong man, with beautiful features and ... her mouth nearly gaped until she caught it. "Abraham." Her skin prickled from shoulders to toes.

He gave her a light bow and soft grin, very soft, his eyes peering deeply into hers. "Miss Laerty." His voice was formal.

Maura realized what she'd done and felt a cringe in her stomach. She's used his given name. He didn't seem to mind although several volunteers and staff stared. She brushed at her hair with fingers reddened and dry from scrubbing and wished she had listened to Miss Jeanne and at least fixed herself a bit.

He stepped closer, his arms stiffly behind his back. His stance highlighted his muscular build, the straight shoulders, the ... the incredible green eyes. "I owe you great thanks, I believe, for your warm care of Mr. Terry's children. I am here..." He ducked his head slightly, as if in apology. "As the will said, I am to take responsibility for their raising. I do hope ... as I have no experience with infants..." He looked around at the cribs nearby.

"She is in the next room. I will call for someone to bring her." Before she had a chance, one of the girls ran off to find Samantha.

Abraham stared. Maura tried to find something to say. "You owe me nothing. It has been a joy." Her voice caught. She pushed at her hair again. "I apologize. You caught me off-guard and I'm afraid I'm quite a mess."

His head tilted as he studied her and he took several steps closer. "You are the loveliest sight I have seen in a very long time, and I am happy to take you as you are." A glint reflected in his eyes as he pulled a small bouquet of wildflowers from behind his back. "Owed or not, I am grateful. I know it has been a struggle. I wish to do what I can to ease your burdens now, of my own volition, not as a repaid debt."

Her jaw dropped. She barely had time to raise it again before the girl came with Samantha and the baby lunged for her. Maura stroked her hair. "Look here, baby." She glanced up as Abraham moved closer. "This is your father now. You are ... you will do well with his guidance." She had trouble getting the words out. Maura knew it would be hard when the time came to hand her over, but she didn't imagine it would be quite so hard. The baby studied him. Abraham continued to close the distance until Maura could nearly feel his warmth.

He took Samantha's pudgy hand. "You are a beautiful child.

Cameron would be proud." His eyes watered the tiniest bit as they rose to Maura's. "I will do my best to be a good father."

Maura wanted to pull him in. She wanted to touch his face, to tell him she had no doubt he would be. Any fear she had that she may not have enough attraction to him in person dissipated into how horribly she wanted to take him in her arms. Instead, she accepted the flowers with thanks, pulled them out of Samantha's attempted grasp, and asked one of the girls to put them in water. "You may as well begin to get acquainted." She handed him the baby. There was no objection from either.

Maura had to turn away. Samantha was hers. By all rights, she was her child. It was unfair ... but Abraham would be able to care for her better. With assistance, which he could easily find with all the young women who would flock to him, as they were doing already right there in the home, offering baby care service as he needed. She knew they had much more in mind than that. And they looked less tired. Younger. Fresher.

"Miss Laerty?"

She bit her lip at Abraham's voice. It was impolite to turn away. She gathered herself as she'd had so much practice doing over the past several months, and gave him a weak grin as she turned. "She seems to think you will be fine as a father. She doesn't often go to strangers. Not that ... I shouldn't have called you a stranger. I only meant..."

"Maura."

She raised her eyes to his at his use of her first name.

"I do not intend to take her from you. She is more yours than mine. As I said in my letter, the one I should not have sent and meant not to let go, I would like you to remain as her ... as her mother, which, by all rights, you are."

"But ... are you moving back to the farm? I was sure you would, as you love it so."

"Yes. I have been there already. Our animals are returned where they should be and winter crops will go in soon."

She nodded. "And you should have someone to care for your children as you work, someone..."

"Yes. As soon as I have it in more livable condition. When it is fit for a lady, it shall, I hope, have one to make it a real home again."

Maura swallowed and pulled her eyes away. A lady. From what she had seen in the area recently, she figured he might have to travel a bit in order to find one. They had only working women now and grieving widows and young girls not fit to be wives and mothers yet, and the few girls barely old enough, several of which hovered around him at this moment.

"I do hope it will not take me long to restore it to such condition. In the meantime…"

She looked back at him. "Oh, but a lady worth having wouldn't throw such a fuss. For a farm in restoration, I would think you do not want someone so particular. You should have someone willing to work beside you…" She felt heat rise into her cheeks at the amusement on his face. "I am sorry. That was not my place."

He leaned forward the slightest bit, his voice lowered. "Possibly it is your place." He shifted Samantha in his arm and again tilted his head, studying her. "Would you perhaps know a lady who would be willing to take the farm, and myself, as we are?"

The oldest girl nearby said she was willing; she was a hard worker and enjoyed being outdoors, which annoyed her mother to no end. Another said she was better with gardens and also loved children.

"Maura?" He cut off their prattle.

She refused to answer, or to meet his eyes. She would not help him find another girl. She would do most anything to help him, but she would not do that. "I am sure you will have no trouble on that end."

After a moment of silence, he took a step backward. "So then, my request from the letter still stands. I will take Rudy with me and we will fix up the farm. My father says he will stay in town and help watch over Samantha until such time as I can manage with her. That is, if you will allow them to continue to stay with you."

"As long as they wish."

"Very well." His voice returned to formal, rigid. "If you won't mind, we'll take the baby with us for the day while you have work here. Rudy was about to introduce me to the new diner in town. Of course you are welcome to join us if you are able."

Maura caught Rudy standing to one side, and Abraham's father. Had they been there the whole time?

"We have worked her hard enough for today." Miss Jeanne touched her back. "Go on now. Help the baby get acquainted. She will be more comfortable."

"Oh, but…"

Abraham turned to hand Samantha to Rudy as she reached for the boy. He grimaced when she jerked against his left shoulder. He had been injured. She was uncertain how badly but after this much time, it had to be an awful wound to still bother him, or it had not been cared for well enough.

"Your injury was in your shoulder?"

He caught her eyes. "It was, but it is healing and will be well."

"It doesn't look to be well enough yet. Did you receive proper care?"

"As well as they could manage. There were worse injured who needed more attention."

Maura frowned and took his arm. "Stretch it to your side." At his hesitation, she became annoyed. "I am well trained by now to deal with injuries and wounds of all kinds. Do as I say." He didn't raise it higher than forty-five degrees and that was a struggle. It was not healing well enough. "Come. Take off that jacket and let me look."

"Miss Laerty…"

"Do not argue. I am also well used to men who believe they have no need of a woman's care and I have no further patience for it. You will have a hard time fixing up that farm and taking care of two children without proper use of the shoulder. Come." She led him toward a chair and began to pull at the jacket buttons.

"I can manage that."

She stood back and allowed him to remove it on his own. One of the girls took it out of the way. "Sit." She was nearly surprised when he obeyed. "Can you manage to also unbutton the shirt? I cannot see the wound through the sleeves."

"I do not believe this is necessary. As I said…"

"I believe it is. Do you or do I? Unless you would rather I have one of the other assistants…"

He asked for more privacy, with a glance at the girls who still swarmed. Maura sent them away and pulled the sheet half closed. She would not fully close them off together.

Abraham unbuttoned the shirt, starting from the top, the one at his wrist last. She helped pull it away from his shoulder. He took it all the way off his arm, leaving half his upper torso fully uncovered. Maura had to clench her teeth at the sight of so much of his skin. He wouldn't have needed to pull it so far off. He had to know he didn't. Still, she'd seen many injured soldiers so uncovered, even more than this. It only slightly bothered her in the beginning, an embarrassment only, not … not this. He was beautiful. Firm. Trim. Muscular, but not overdone. She was glad to have sent the other girls away. She didn't want to share him so much.

The thought made her face start to warm and she focused on the large bandage. "It at least looks clean."

"As it is. I change it twice a day to rinse off the old blood."

"It bleeds still?"

"At times. It is a large wound. Perhaps another should look instead?"

"You think I cannot handle the sight of blood and wounds after all these months I've worked here? I am not that weak, Mr. Luchner." She began to ease the edges of the bandage off skin too fragile from being covered for so long. His eyes were on her. Watching for weakness, she supposed. He would find none.

She winced at the sight of the long, deep slash and scolded herself. Some of the stitches had pulled away. Overuse, from the look of it. Otherwise, the job seemed done well. "You are using it too often, or too strenuously."

"There has, at times, been little choice."

Maura met his eyes. "They should have sent you home earlier."

"They tried."

"What?"

"I refused to leave, until my farm was threatened."

She bit her tongue, nodded, and called for one of the girls to bring whatever medic was free. "It will need to be re-stitched where they've pulled. Infection will set in otherwise, particularly if you insist on working right away, which I'm afraid you will."

"I have little choice."

"You should hire help."

"I'm afraid all of the funds I have will need to go directly into supplies, to food for the animals, and ourselves, until we are resettled." He grasped her hand when she started out to gather what she knew the medic would need. "Maura, granted I have little to offer. However..."

Doctor McGovern entered with a clearing of his throat. "Pardon the interruption. My medics are involved elsewhere, and as I was informed the patient was our own Sergeant Luchner, I decided to see what the lad needs myself. Good to have you home. Your father is a new man again." He peered at the wound. "Miss Laerty, you were correct in calling me, as always. We'll have to fix this. Fetch a small amount of whatever pain relief we still have..."

"It's unnecessary." Abraham pulled his chin up. "Save it for those who need it more."

Maura began to object.

"The first time it was stitched, I had none, and this is minor in comparison. I do have urgent matters to attend, so if we can take care of this quickly, I would be grateful."

"Urgent? I believe you were headed to the diner."

"Yes, Mr. Rudy will be beside himself with hunger soon. We cannot have that."

She grinned, despite herself, despite the way her eyes continued to fall to his chest beyond her control, despite the pain he was about to subject himself to which hurt her stomach.

"Well, then." The doctor moved his glance between the two of them. "Go and fetch a full shot of my personal sedative and bring it to the lad. If we cannot stop the pain, we can at least make him less worried about it." He gave her a wink and began to retrieve his tools of the trade.

Abraham grimaced at times as he was stitched, but said nothing and otherwise kept his face even. Maura wished she'd taken some of the whiskey for herself, as it appeared to bother her more than it did him. Proper or not, she took his hand and set her other on his good shoulder as soon as the doctor no longer required her assistance.

"That should do it, and I do expect my work to be respected, Abe." The doctor set his tools to the side. "Easy on that until you come back to see me in ten days and we'll see how it's doing. Miss Laerty, kindly bandage it up again before you let him bolt."

She gave a nod and gathered a fresh bandage as Abraham thanked his father's friend and invited him to dinner as soon as they were up to having company. And they were alone again.

Maura first cleaned the remaining blood from the outside of the wound. She realized she touched his skin far more than necessary and yet did nothing to change that. Silence remained between them while she covered it, the bandage larger than the last in order to avoid taping over skin already tender. She smoothed the tape as well as she could, more than she needed. His warmth seeped into her fingers, her palm. A fleeting thought of allowing her hand to roam farther quickened her pulse.

"You didn't answer my last letter."

Her palm froze against his skin. She met his eyes. "It was intercepted."

"I'm sorry?"

"It seems … there has been talk about us, and … and I should leave now and let you dress."

He grasped her hand before she could get far from him. "Intercepted, how?"

"By the same thief who broke into my house to find your earlier letters. Before I saw it, even. I only read it the other day when your father went to retrieve the whole bunch of them."

"He read it?"

"No. It was unopened by some miracle. Abraham…"

He stood, his body far too close to hers, still half uncovered. He paid no mind to the way his bare skin beckoned to her, made her pulse race, her cheeks flush. It was too inappropriate, even if he was injured, if she was helping him as she had so many others.

He touched one of the unruly strands of hair falling alongside her face and she clenched her eyes.

"Maura, the letter was written under effects of a concussion and grief. I was not myself, and yet…"

"I will hold you to nothing you said. I have not shared a word of it."

"You wish not to hold me to my words?" His fingers moved to her face.

"I wish … oh, Abraham, you mustn't." Her skin prickled all the way to her toes.

"Are you betrothed to another?"

"No." She met his eyes. "No, there is no other. Never. I have yet so much as to accept even a light kiss from a suitor, of which there have been very few. I am too much … of my own mind, so my father said."

"Not so much as a kiss?"

"Never."

"And if I were to undo that?"

"Oh." She bit her lip and wondered how to ask him to please undo it without allowing herself to sound too unlike a lady. "I believe Rudy awaits a meal. The boy eats all day if I allow." Maura reached to grasp his shirt and pull it around, holding it until he slid his arm in the sleeve. She straightened the front and began to do his buttons, from the bottom.

"Will you allow me to court you? As I started to say…." He grasped her hands. "I have little to offer, other than the children you love already. I am a hard worker, and determined, however, and the farm will return to its glory, well enough to be a good support."

"I am not searching for support of that kind. What I wish for…"

He leaned closer. "You wish to walk outside without your

parasol, to work the earth without reprisal for dirt on your fingers, to care for another and to have care given you in return, to support and also to be supported, to love truly and be loved truly. You wish to be in a place of your choosing, not one thrust upon you."

Moistness tinged her eyes. "How do you know all that?"

"From your letters. I can offer you that, in the least, all but the loving truly. I can only offer what I am and the chance to find out whether you might ever feel enough for me to consider the rest."

"Are you offering yourself to me, Sergeant Luchner?"

He lowered his face and claimed her lips. It was a sweet kiss, soft, forceful and yielding all at once. An offer. In his kiss, she felt an offer of much, much more. His breath was heavier upon release, his body still nearly meshed with hers. "Yes, Miss Laerty. I offer myself to you, if you will have me."

If she would have him. With a light smile, she reached up to his mouth, returning the claim. Proper or not, Maura released his hands and slid hers around his back, beneath the loosely hanging shirt. He pulled her in, his own hand on her back, the other behind her head.

"Well, you had better accept him after a kiss like that." Miss Jeanne's voice scolded with a teasing tone. "No one else will have you after such a display."

Abraham pulled back enough to touch Maura's eyes. "And no one else best try." He asked for his jacket, waited until it was retrieved to pull something from a pocket, and lowered to one knee. He grasped her fingers, looking over just for a moment when Miss Jeanne opened the curtain full. "Maura, every word you wrote built my strength enough to continue my duty through days I would otherwise have been fully willing to walk away with the slightest push. On my way home, a man called me a hero, while others called me evil. I am neither. I am no more and no less than a simple farmer and proud to be such. I am loyal, hardworking, and fully devoted to whatever I give my interest. I am a father by fate, left to me by the man who gave his life to save mine." He paused, dropped his eyes.

"Abraham?" Maura touched his right shoulder.

He returned his gaze. "I did not deserve such an honor but his children will be well loved by me, well cared for, and will inherit my land equally along with any children I might have of my own. They do need a mother, one who will treat them the same, who will love them the same. Maura, although I know you love them already, I do not ask for your hand because of the children, but because of my own needs. I fell in love with you through your letters. They helped to bring me home again. And although I also do not deserve the honor of your agreement to be my wife, I ask if you will."

"Yes." Maura touched his face. "Abraham, yes. And it will be my honor. I do want you to know, I am not accepting because of the children. I am accepting because I see in you everything I have looked for." She raised her fingers to his hair, the light brown shiny hair she'd fallen for from a distance so long ago. Before they'd met. Before the war. Before the letters.

"And I, in you." He slid the ring on her finger, kissed her hand, and stood.

With a hand closing around the back of her head, he took her mouth again. She heard whispers around them, gasps of disbelief, and it didn't matter. Her Abraham was home.

The longing in his eyes when they touched hers again shook her to her soul's depths. It wasn't the way Cameron had looked at her, or any other male who had tried for her attention. It wasn't lustful in its desire, but genuine, whole.

He ran a thumb across her cheek. "I will work from dawn to dusk to ready the farm so you can join me as soon as we're married. I do wish it to be soon."

"Marry me today and take me home with you. I will work at your side."

He seemed unsure whether to laugh or kiss her again. "I could not ask it…"

"You are not. I am offering. I am asking you. I have only kept the house to have a roof over our heads. I have no wish to remain in it. It should sell easily. The money can go into the farm. Besides, someone must see to it you do not overdo your shoulder before it heals." She stroked a hand lightly just below the wound.

"I was afraid I misspoke with that last letter."

"No. My Abraham, you could never misspeak. Not to me. I loved every word you wrote. I even loved the words you did not write I could sense you withholding. You needn't withhold any words with me."

His eyes caressed her face. He pulled her in closer. "Today is nearly over. I wish us to have dinner and talk on the eve of our engagement. You may change your mind after an amount of time in my actual presence."

"I will not. Perhaps, though, today is too soon. And I am far too disordered…"

"You are beautiful." He raised her hand to kiss her fingers.

"And I shall have a hard time waiting any longer for you, so perhaps ... if it is possible ... we could marry tomorrow, in the morning, before I allow you too much time to regain your senses."

"Or your own." Maura reminded herself, even as her hand slid down onto his chest and her mouth touched his, allowing him to deepen the kiss, to pull her in, that they were not alone, that the girls and some of the patients and his father were there...

"It is not only possible; it seems to be necessary." His father, behind them, to their side, teased. "Come Rudy, find the stroller and let's hurry to the minister and begin the arrangements. Is there a certain place you wish to hold a wedding?"

Maura held Abraham's eyes. "The canyon."

He grinned. "Yes. At sunrise."

"Yes."

Abraham lay at his wife's side and stroked her bare skin as she slept. Much of the town had turned out for the wedding and celebrations had kept him at too much distance from her for much of the day. Their first night spent on the farm, at their home, while his father kept the children in town, was to be followed by a brief honeymoon in the mountains. It was early October, warm enough still, with enough preparation. They would keep each other warm. The cold, when it came, would never again penetrate him as it had the past winter.

On their return, they would retrieve whatever she wished to take from her father's house. There was a buyer already. Several offered during the day. She made a good deal on it with Cameron's youngest brother who had a beau already and wished for a house big enough for the many children they wanted. He was the only one of the Terrys to attend the wedding. His apology for his family was combined with his wish to be an uncle to Samantha. Abe readily agreed.

There was much work to be done and Maura insisted the house sale go toward the work, partly toward hiring help until he was better healed. She was determined to work at his side, as much as she could around Samantha, at least until they began to extend their family. The first order of business along with winter crops would be to fix up the guest house. His father insisted he would move into it to allow their privacy. Abe also planned to build onto the main house. They took no precautions while together and neither wanted precautions. They wanted children. At least two more.

He kissed her shoulder and she started; her eyes opened. "I did not mean to wake you."

She smiled and slid a hand over his chest. "I am glad you did. I did not mean to fall asleep so soon."

"It has been a long day. You should sleep."

"No. The last year and a half were terribly long. Today was terribly short and I do not wish it to end yet."

"No?" He turned her onto her back. "Then it will not."

Maura pulled him closer. "You are my hero, Abraham." She whispered beside his ear.

He kissed her deeply and snuggled down against her bare skin. "You give me reason to be."

+_+_+   Spring   +_+_+

(many years later)

epilogue

My Dear Grandchildren, and all the greats present and future,

I write this as a preface of sorts to go along with the various sketches and photos of my artistic work that our dear Samantha vows to have bound into some sort of compilation. It is of her bidding, not my own, as I fail to see first, the need to bind and spread my simple works created only out of keeping my fingers useful in some way, and second, what my words could possibly add. She is quite the insistent child, however, and so I give in to the request. Never mind the shakiness of these scratchings. Years of dealing with insistent and outrageous children and grandchildren have pulled the steadiness right out of me. A good thing, it is, that your Grandma Maura is still steady as the rock she has always been. If Rudy has gathered all the tales of our origins and life as he says, to go along with the compilation, you will know already of my dear wife and what a true Godsend she has always been to me, and is still.

Ours was not the easiest of lives, although perhaps there is no such thing and we spend far too much time considering the possibility that there could be. Regardless, there is only one moment I would change, and that would be to have brought Samantha's father of the biological kind back with me from that war that, as I see from the perspective of the years, cured so many more evils than it caused. I hear tell of the possibility of another and shed an occasional tear for the thought of any of you caught up in it, which will be all of you in some way or another. They are not fully sad tears, mind you, but also tears of pride for the way I know you shall stand up with your principles and fulfill your duties and do your best in whatever role comes for you. Know wherever I am, I shall watch over you and shall always be with you in some spirit.

I should come to the point of what Samantha has asked of me: a bit of an explanation about some of my work. I am unsure how to go about the task, but where to start is a simple thing.

A pair of bed stands, crudely made and carved, now adorns each side of Samantha's four poster. It is where they should be and it will be up to her where they go next, other than on a bonfire which would be their rightful place if not for the story behind them. It is the exact pair that distracted me from each day's events as I worked on them while away overseas, with dear Cameron Terry as my tent mate. One was his and depicts parts of his life, and one mine. Those, and the letters Maura saved that he wrote, seemed helpful in connecting Samantha to her father through the years, along with the stories his youngest brother, Uncle Alex, insisted on telling, despite Cameron being unable to defend himself against them. I did my best to preserve his honor. Although, truth be told, his honor held its own without my assistance.

Cameron's family moved away quite soon after Maura and I settled in together. It was no great loss, as Alex himself often said. I have forever been grateful for Alex, who stood beside his brother, my friend, against the rest. In turn, we took him in as our family and have been all the better for having him. He was quite the help in restoring this old farm while I recovered from my shoulder injury.

Enough of that, I suppose, since Rudy has likely written that part of our history already. On to my own task:

Maura insists I should speak of the chairs next, while she reads my scratches over my shoulder. She always did love to scour the words I put in print, perhaps more than she paid heed to those I said aloud. That was a little jest, a common joke between us, since it was our letters that brought us together.

The chairs: There are a set of four wooden folding

chairs that I also wasted valuable time engraving for no obvious reason other than that Maura wished it. They echo a gift I was consigned to do once. She saw the gift and dare thought she should have her own. I have never had reason to want to turn her down for anything she asked, and so, here they are. They belong to Rudy now, as he spent so much time lugging them to the canyon and back to prevent us older folks from being unable to get up off the blanket after picnicking. They depict the four seasons. Why I decided on that theme, I couldn't say.

The sketches that match, drawn with nothing but charcoal, are in the hands of Jeanne, the first born of Maura and myself. Named after ... well now I am sure Rudy has covered that, as well. Jeanne shares my love of simple nature sketches of charcoal and while some of the others might ask for a story at night, our little artist in her own right would hand me paper and charcoal and ask me for a story-scene, as she took to calling them: a little piece of something in my past, or in her mother's past. She would then take it carefully by the edges and pin it to her wall. If the little holes still show all over the third bedroom, now you will know why they are there.

To Louis Cameron go the sketches I did while away on duty, in honor of his own military service in which he excelled, was decorated, and is now home again. Louis, despite his name, is his mother's child through and through. His fingers have always been dirty, his heart has always been in helping others, and behind the façade of propriety and politeness runs a wicked stubborn streak that has served them both well. Also to our young hero goes all of what remains of my engraving tools and my drawing supplies. I have the utmost confidence they will be put to better use than what I have done.

Josiah: anything I have done with color involved stems from our Josiah, named for Maura's father. With each carving or sketch I finished, Joe asked why the colors were missing. It was never right without color, since everything had it. So then, I am afraid my earliest attempts at watercolor have been saved instead of burned. You can directly blame Joe for them, and leave them all to him. The little animal depicted in so many colored images I drew of running Joey – always at odds with his mother's attempts to turn him into a gentleman – was a scrappy little dog he found and adopted, much to the detriment of several of my slippers and Maura's linens.

Dear Charles: to the marksman of the bunch who took no greater pleasure in anything than he did in hitting the center of a target at unbelievable distances, goes his grandfather's Colt. Charles, who we still rarely see due to his ongoing career service, reminds me much of myself in his lack of communication and makes me glad to have relented while away from my own father. A joy with sparkling eyes, the lad will do great things in years to come. I also leave him the remainder of my writing paper and ink pens, as a reminder that wherever he runs, his family is never farther away than a letter.

To little Allison Maureen, and she will roll her eyes as she reads I still call her this for all posterity to see, belongs the old swing with the carving of the hands and home. She spent many hours entertaining her grandfather as he rocked outside in the yard looking out over the property. Her little fingers often traced the carving, which was a gift to my dear father as I left for duty, in the case I did not return. As his eyesight weakened, she piled book after book at her side and read and reread his favorites and hers. It is of no curiosity to me that Allison set her path to teaching children to read who were kept at home to work instead of attending school. You will, I believe, find sketches here and there showing Allison beside her grandfather on that old swing.

My dearest Maura reminds me that this was to be about my art and instead reads as a will. She is perhaps right that Samantha will ask me to try again. I ask, however, how my art could possibly be about more than my wife and my children and the wonderful life I wish to pass along to them, to remind them of. That is the basis for what I create. It instills meaning into everything I do. What I leave behind speaks more volumes than anything else I can say. Our children are the greatest creativity I could have hoped to have part in. Parenting is, after all, a work in progress, an art form of light and shadows, of perspective and of colors and shades. The same can be said of all life. Art may indeed be a poor imitation of actual life, but what else, I pray, are we able to truly leave behind? Perhaps it is more about what is left behind than about our reasons for creating whatever it is we create.

With that, I close this letter and shall go out to the old bench where Maura awaits my company to watch the sun set together, as has become our habit. I leave you, those who will remember me and those who are too young or have not yet come, with one wish:

Whatever life brings to you, whatever battles you choose to fight or to refuse, there is one thing that matters above all. Guard what is within your heart, for that will show in what you leave behind more than any other thing in this world.

With my best and kindest regards,
Abraham Luchner

Protect The Heart
by Catherine Moore

Please listen to my letters
and read between the lines
my heart is stained in ink curves
of what is written, and words
protected off page.

Please look inside my drawings
of secluded scenery, my
heart is hidden in crevices
of artfully charcoaled
Ansel Adam landscapes.

Please find my words poetic
though discreet in presentation
this language merely
a layered propriety
confined upon my soul.

Please feel the warmth in this sketch
as frozen prairie grasses thaw
in the tender light of seasons
where new life bounds, confined
behind barb-wire fences.

Please hear the cry in this message
bold as a newborn's breath
it carries the needs and dreams
of women and men, swaddled
in lines bound womb-tight.

Please touch the hearth drawn
with its blazing fire in my homestead
a burning dream which will remain
under paper moon and mountains
unless you believe them true.

Catherine Moore is a freelance writer and poet. A "scribbler" since they handed her a pencil as a child, after graduating from the Florida State University with a degree in English Literature she has spent most of her career working in education and public relations fields. Catherine is an avid traveler and has visited 14 different countries, including living overseas at the age of four. A literacy advocate, she volunteers as an ESOL tutor at her local public library. Catherine has also placed in Area and Regional speech competitions with Toastmasters Club, Intl. She is a Preferred Author at Writing.Com, which is listed in Writer's Digest as one of the 101 Best Websites for Writers.

Some of Catherine's recent publications include short stories and poems in *Six Little Things*, *MaMaZina* Magazine, *Emerald Tales*, and others.

This story was a last-minute surprise pulled out of a helmet.

When I start a new book, I have already pondered it months or years in advance. I know the characters inside and out. The plot is well-formed in my head. I may or may not have some notes written here and there, but all major events have been pre-written before I ever touch paper or keyboard. Not so with this one. As *Nanowrimo approached and I was getting set up for a one month whirlwind every-other-day-post blog tour for my just-released *Off The Moon*, I realized I would have to have something to write 50,000 words *about.* At the end of October, I grabbed onto a faint idea of a war story of sorts and by November 1st, three characters had slightly appeared. With only first names and an idea of their story, I jumped in fingers first. It flowed right out as though it had been waiting for me to get to it for years. Maybe it had.

They say to write what you know. As the spouse of a now-retired career soldier, I did that to a great extent with this book.

Abraham was the first character to come to mind. He is, however, the secondary character. It is Maura's story. It may seem odd to the reader to focus so highly on Abe, then, but any military wife knows that's how it works: even in her own life story, the largest focus is on her spouse. The military is not simply a job. It is a lifestyle everything else must work around, to a whole different extent than any other career. Telling the Army, "No, I won't move to the very edge of hell" doesn't work. They say where, you ask when. So, to tell Maura's story any other way than firmly around Abraham would be unrealistic.

I managed 52,000 words in November, which made a complete first draft. In March, I did the major rewrite: filling in, rearranging, adding detail, plus another 12,000 words more or less. By the end of March, it was down to the detail edits and the sketches. The charcoal sketches became a necessity to finish the thing as it needed. It had been years since I worked with charcoal, although I used to often sit outside in my grandparents' big tree- and flower-filled yard or at the window looking out at it and jot down what I saw with a charcoal stick, and later charcoal pencils. It's quite an expressive medium. It's particularly good for trees and has a nice, old-fashioned feel.

The setting is a tribute to my own soldier-hero, my husband. The cover photos were taken years before on a visit to his home state. It is a gorgeous place that left a lasting impression each time I saw it. Where else should I put Abraham but there?

The old-time feel when ladies and gentlemen were expected to be such is a tribute to my great uncles who served so valiantly, one of whom was lost in war before I could meet him. To Max, then. And Harold and Hal and John. And to their families who held the pieces together at home.

To all who have served or are still serving: Thank You and God Bless.

LK Hunsaker

*Nanowrimo.org – the quest to write 50,000 words of a new novel during the 30 days of November. No need to be an author to join, just come play!

My website: www.LKHunsaker.com

Just ere the closing of the day,
My dying couch I then would have
Borne out in the refreshing air,
Where sweet shrubs grow and proud trees
wave.

Walt Whitman
from "My Departure"

www.ingramcontent.com/pod-product-compliance
Lightning Source LLC
Chambersburg PA
CBHW020328110726
47898CB00003B/797